# PEOPLE COLLIDE

# PEOPLE COLLIDE

A NOVEL

# ISLE McELROY

 HARPERVIA

An Imprint of HarperCollins*Publishers*

PEOPLE COLLIDE. Copyright © 2023 by Isle McElroy. All rights reserved. Printed in the United States of America. No part of this book may be used or reproduced in any manner whatsoever without written permission except in the case of brief quotations embodied in critical articles and reviews. For information, address HarperCollins Publishers, 195 Broadway, New York, NY 10007.

HarperCollins books may be purchased for educational, business, or sales promotional use. For information, please email the Special Markets Department at SPsales@harpercollins.com.

First HarperVia hardcover published in 2023

FIRST EDITION

Designed by Janet Evans-Scanlon

Title page and part opener art © profartshop/Shutterstock

Library of Congress Cataloging-in-Publication Data is available upon request.

ISBN 978-0-06-328375-6

23 24 25 26 27  LBC  5 4 3 2 1

*For my mom*

PART I

I am not a responsible man. I am not a brave man—which is not to say I am a coward. But no one would ever consider me brave. My wife, Elizabeth, was the brave one. She was why we were living abroad for a year, in a small city in southern Bulgaria, a country known for its tomatoes and yogurt and for having balanced on the fingertip of the Soviet Union.

Each day, however, is a chance to discard your most pitiable habits and selves. Especially this day, a Friday, the day of the week devoted to transitions, to sloughing off and forgetting. When I stepped outside into the grand street in front of my apartment complex, I found, before me, a chance to become someone better: a hero. A cat lay dead in the street, splayed on the pavement in front of a dumpster. A kitten. Soggy from a morning thunderstorm that had only recently passed. No one around seemed to notice the cat. The men in track jackets and acid-washed jeans, the grandmothers hauling plastic sacks of tomatoes and greens, the dignified grandfathers in time-wrinkled suits strutting with their hands clasped behind their backs. They passed the cat without looking down.

Strays were not rare in the city. Entire families of kittens often spilled out from under dumpsters or crowded the back doors of butcher shops. Throughout the city, stray cats were feted with paper plates full of kibble and saucers of milk and scratch after scratch on the head. Living here for three months had made obvious my own embarrassing American impulse to act entirely out of self-interest, as opposed to my Bulgarian friends, who walked a cautious line between cynicism and care—and thus they were generous without expectations. Americans were puppets of their ambitions, obsessed with taking part in their own lives, in knowing themselves, in doing, in being, in living, in fundamentally changing the world, all in the service of our own egos. My friends' cynicism was a nice counterpoint to this impulse. It seemed borne on a true understanding of life: Very little we ever did mattered. Our only requirement was to keep moving. Outside, on a bench in the park across from my apartment building, two old men sat beside each other, as still and silent as snow.

Sometimes even moving is too much.

That day, however, I wanted to be my truest American self. I felt compelled—and I never felt compelled—to do right by the cat in the street. After seeing the cat, I spun around and wrenched open the front door to my apartment building. We lived on the top floor of a charmless five-story apartment complex; it was the newest building on our block, the exterior as blank as bone. The inside flooring was faux marble and scuffed. The walls were hospital gray, inhospitably gray. There was an elevator, big enough for three people, max, but I never used it.

I preferred punishing myself—though instead of using a word like *punishing*, I deployed phrases like *pushing my limits* and *staying in shape*, because I never liked to admit to my unhealthy obsessions.

A thin, difficult man in a blue track jacket smoking a cigarette paced in the lobby. Desi and Kiril, two friends who owned a café around the corner, insisted that this man was a mobster, though they never said so without laughing, and I couldn't tell whether they were playing a joke on me. He spent his days smoking in front of the building, grumbling into his phone, trading hand-shakes with nervous young men. A week into our stay, Elizabeth and I had offered him a single square of baklava—we had ac-cidentally come into a tray's worth, too much for two—and he accepted, reluctantly and confused. I believed that this made us friends.

I nodded at him. He ignored me. I climbed the steps two at a time—staying in shape. Curved bay windows were built into every landing. On each floor, I peered out the window to see if anyone had moved the kitten. Floor two: No one had moved the kitten. Floor three: No one had moved the kitten. Floor four: No one had moved the kitten. Floor five: No one had moved the kitten. I unlocked the door to our apartment: a thick pie slice of a studio stuffed between the elevator and a much larger apartment. I grabbed a plastic bag from under the sink and checked to ensure every burner was off, then glimpsed out the sliding glass door that opened onto a shared balcony. Behind the apartment stood the charred remains of an old house, and during the sunniest parts of the day, a trim tabby would perch on the beams, licking its paws. If I sound like I am obsessing over the cats in this city, it is because I am. The routines of the cats brought order and joy to my depressing existence. I waved to the cat—which I called Fire Cat, for obvious reasons—then scampered back to the steps.

On the ground floor, I nodded at my neighbor again and—minor miracle—he lifted his head. It was the opening to a nod, I believed, but he kept tilting his face to the ceiling, inspecting the landing above him, from which water had begun to drip.

"Goodbye," I said in Bulgarian.

Outside was chilly and wet. I wrapped the plastic bag over my hand and crossed the street to the dumpster, but when I crouched to scoop up the kitten, it yawned awake and fled under the dumpster to sit with its siblings. Their eyes mooned out from the dark. I stood up, stuck with the fork of disbelief, until a passerby tossed a black bag in the trash.

My little bout of heroism made me late to meet Elizabeth at the school where she taught. She led lessons on American culture for teenagers who, even at their most invested, found her indoctrinating lessons taxing and ridiculous. The teaching position was sponsored by the American government, and many of its past recipients had gone on to hold stable government jobs withholding aid from developing nations. Everyone who learned of her appointment cooed with admiration.

The illustriousness of the job and its promise of future employment wreaking havoc abroad in the name of American interests prevented the fellows from admitting that the work they performed primarily sucked. They were underpaid and under-respected by students, and by the Bulgarian teachers assigned to serve as their mentors. The only way to maintain something like self-worth in the face of such disrespect was to adopt a condescending distaste for Bulgaria and its people. Elizabeth and I considered ourselves above such condescension. Rather, she was above it, too intelligent and empathetic to succumb to such simplistic and racist thinking, whereas I considered myself below this condescension, too much of nothing to regard myself better than anyone else. I was not here because I had earned my way here. I was here because Elizabeth loved me. When she received the fellowship offer, she and I were not married. We chose to get married—to each other—so I could join her abroad. This isn't to say we didn't love each other; we had been dating for three years. However, in our marriage, love came secondary to the bureaucratic convenience that marriage provided.

Though no one ever marries for love. They marry for weddings. They marry for money. They marry for clout. They marry to make children of married parents. We married to take advantage of a system. No matter how much Elizabeth loved me—and we told each other every day, deep, honest expressions of love, looking-you-in-the-eyes kind of statements—I could never shake the sense that I was, for her, like a supplementary arm grafted onto the center of her stomach. Occasionally, the limb would prove helpful, say, when she needed to hold a third cup or haul something heavy, but most days the limb was an obstruction, a severely noticeable appendage that people treated with kindness and respect to hide their concern.

To combat this sense of helplessness, I joined Elizabeth at her school for the final two periods of class every day to assist her in teaching. She did not have an assistant teacher during this stretch. I offered little pedagogical aid, though she seemed to appreciate my presence. At best, I diluted the attention directed at her. As an irresponsible person, I, with no expectation of future government work, cracked jokes that Elizabeth couldn't. I made funny noises and faces that disrupted the everyday tensions of imperialism. I knew my place in the world. Though Elizabeth and I were both writers, I lacked ambition and talent. I loved to lounge, I loved to waste time, I loved to treat myself when no treats had been earned.

I loved to be late. Today I was later than normal. On the walk to the school, I adopted the tiring pace I had grown accustomed to, pumping my arms, my legs bounding in a cartoonish combination of walking and jogging. It was unlikely I moved any faster this way, but I needed to try, because that morning, Elizabeth had given me an ultimatum: Either show up on time or don't show up at all. I didn't want to endanger one of the few activities that gave my life some shaving of meaning.

The month was November, already too chilly for what I left the house wearing—jeans and a breezy yellow sweater, no undershirt. My hair hadn't been cut since I arrived, and it hung wetly over my eyes, still undried from the shower I'd taken that morning. I was not the type to care for myself, to put in the effort to style my hair or to apply deodorant or Q-tip my ears, especially not when I was depressed, and after three months in Bulgaria, sharing a pie slice of an apartment, frantically married to the woman I hoped to die alongside—at an appropriately creaky age—I had become recklessly depressed. Stability like ours could cause suffering of the most mundane variety: boredom, perhaps, is the word for this feeling. Marriage had melted our days into one warped single day, like a wax statue burned to a blob. Some people find joy in stability. I have known these people—the accountants and lawyers and truckers and cats—but I was not these people. I grew up in what one former therapist called a "chaotic environment" and now everything nonchaotic felt claustrophobic. I had a tendency, too, according to a later therapist, to unsettle the settled parts of my life, like a child cutting out patches of hair. Perhaps this was why I paused to bury the cat in the dumpster: I was always looking for ways to snip stability out of my life.

I pictured Elizabeth's lips thinning in anger when I barged into the classroom ten minutes late. She would continue teaching as I slugged to the desk to set down my phone. *Mr. Harding has decided to join us*, she would say, or worse, she would say nothing, treating me the way she had threatened to treat me: as if I hadn't shown up at all.

Half a mile from the school, I turned off the main road and onto a paved pathway flanked by playgrounds and grass. This path led to the back entrance of the school. And as I drew closer, I walked against the current of seniors who left on early release. Normally, the students I passed eyed me suspiciously—I stood out here, unmistakably American—but today the seniors kept gossiping and smoking in their pods, and this made me feel like I belonged. I had begun to fit in. Reason enough to start running.

I arrived at the school winded, too nervous to check the time. Inside: echoes. The halls were as empty as rusted trucks. I raced to the classroom where Elizabeth taught her tenth graders, on the third floor of the building. I caught my breath outside the door—to preserve some hints of dignity—and practiced my excuse. *I found a kitten dying in the street, an innocent little kitten, and I brought it back to life. I saved the life of a kitten!*

Prepared, I peered through the porthole window on the door to gauge Elizabeth's anger before entering. But she wasn't at the head of the classroom. It was her mentor, Miss Valerie, a honey-haired woman with tired eyes and maraschino lipstick. She caught my face in the window and charged toward the door, flung it open.

"Where have you been?" Less a question than an indictment.

"I got caught up with something urgent," I told her. Miss Valerie scared me in the way every person in power scared me. She didn't love me and thus had no reason to overlook my flaws. To her, I was what I was: a talentless arm attached to a talented stomach.

"Urgent matters don't take all day," she said.

We stood in the doorway, each of us with one leg in the classroom, one out. The students normally used every free minute of distraction to their advantage. But today, they gazed at us, mesmerized, their phones untouched in their laps.

I craned my head around to check the clock above the entrance. "I'm only five minutes late," I said. "Not even."

"Pff," she said.

"Have Elizabeth tell you," I said. "I'm always a little late. I join her when I can." I'd been too flustered to ask where Elizabeth was, and before I could, Miss Valerie raised her voice.

"There is no time for this nonsense," she said. "You don't show up all day to your job—your very important job—and now you are telling me to have *you* tell me where you were. This is some kind of joke."

"Where is Elizabeth?" I asked, worried now for her safety. "Is she coming back soon?"

"I have been covering for you all day and your first words should be *Thank you*." She sped to the desk and retrieved her purse, a leather pouch the size of a globe. "We will talk after class."

"Where is Elizabeth?" I asked again.

"Oh," she said. Something had clicked for her.

"Did she go home early?"

"You are not well," Miss Valerie said.

"I'm as confused as you are," I said. I looked at my hands for grounding, for something familiar, and they were familiar, so very familiar, but the hands were not mine.

Miss Valerie addressed the students in Bulgarian. A few of them let out muffled cheers, but Miss Valerie shushed them. They stuffed their books in their backpacks. They gathered their phones. They filed past me at the door.

"Feel better, Miss Elizabeth," the first student said as he passed.

"Feel better, Miss Elizabeth," said the next child, and the next and the next and the next and the next and the next until I was alone in the room with Miss Valerie.

First, a girl was born. She was born in a small town in rural Michigan to parents who knew how to raise her. She was given a name—Elizabeth—and, when traded between the arms of her mother and the arms of her father, gently kissed on the top of the head. Her parents were rigidly dignified people invested in all forms of improvement. Her mother listened to problems professionally. People came to her with stories of egotism and trauma and grief, and she listened and nodded and *hmm*ed. Her father fed the most creative minds in the world. He sustained the brainpower required to nourish artistic success. A photographer in his twenties, he now prepared the meals for artists at an artist retreat.

The parents carried Elizabeth home to a two-story farmhouse in rural Michigan. Their woodsy town served as a way station for Serious Artists working on Serious Projects. The parents liked living close to Serious Art. They wished to raise their daughter inside the blast radius of creation. They raised her with an esteemed and discerning eye about what mattered and didn't, was good and what wasn't, what was true, what was false, powerful, melodramatic, necessary, and tacky. She would be someone important.

Ten months after the girl was born a boy was born in New Jersey to parents unsure what they meant to each other. The parents were married but far from in love, coupled the way gum couples with the underside of a desk. They barely arrived at the hospital the day of the birth, still grasping and packing the required supplies an hour after labor began. The boy was named Elijah—the mother selected the name—to give him a sense of historical worth. The boy was hairy at birth and smelled, according to the father, like peanuts, and though the father couldn't say why he found this disturbing he found it disturbing nevertheless, a reminder of the boy's otherness, until, so unnerved by the scent, the father left his little bud of a family for a woman who lived across town.

The mother was not prepared to raise a boy on her own but had no other choice. Men disappear; their children remain. She'd been told this as a girl, but some things you never believe until they become part of your life. The mother created spreadsheets at a company where she and her colleagues split the years into quarters and worked two hours too late every night. Eli found meaning on the living room floor, sitting before the rippled maw of a projection screen TV. From age two until age seventeen the boy found love in the screen. It was there for him. It watched over him. It met his need for intimacy and attention. His mother was one of those mothers people call *bad* when the accurate description is *busy*. The father was not a bad father but merely a bad father for his only child and—to his credit—he performed a serviceable role stepfathering the children of the woman he married after leaving the mother.

As the boy grew close with the screen, the girl's parents taught her about art and the world. They instilled in her a sense of moral purpose, superiority, passion. They read her brief illustrated biographies about exemplary women like Harriet Tubman and Marie Curie and Frida Kahlo and Amelia Earhart. These women inspired in Elizabeth an appreciation of beauty and justice. At age ten, she started a community cleanup program along the main road in town that expanded into a service where children took out the trash for elderly neighbors. At twelve, she volunteered on the weekends reading to children in hospitals. She made the varsity basketball team as a freshman and started every game until graduation. She had a brother, four years her junior, whom she only playfully teased, not once with a flicker of malice, and on the rare occasions they fought, she prided herself on restoring the peace between them, over a heaping scoop of ice cream or a slice of pizza. At sixteen, she spearheaded voting drives and raised funds for abortion providers. She was a good person, the goodest they came.

She came from a place that valued greatness and knew it. The most Serious Artists in the world produced their Serious Art in her town. The enlightened drank the same water she did. They watched the same sun descend over the very same trees. Greatness did not intimidate her. She existed through the accumulation of achievements: awards and honors and accolades and receptions and merits and plaques hung on her like ornaments on a tree. When the time came, she applied to only the most elite and isolated colleges in the country. These colleges served her the way engines served airplanes, lifting her to esteemed, predictable heights.

In New Jersey, Eli smoked dusty marijuana out of a Diet Pepsi can in his kitchen. He balanced on an exercise ball while playing football video games. Bloc Party's *Silent Alarm* buzzed on repeat over animated tackling sounds. He had friends but not because they valued his humor or charm. He had friends because his mother worked late. When she returned home, she didn't much care what went on in her house. At her house, teenagers drank in the basement on Wednesdays. At her house, teenagers fucked in the bathroom and puked in the bushes. She would enter her house at nine in the evening on the night of a party and carry a takeout meal to her bedroom and sit upright at the foot of the bed, eating and drinking, the TV cranked to its gravelly max to muffle the sound of parties two floors beneath her.

Eli's town was not a town of importance. The closest thing to a thing that ever happened in town was the filming of a summer camp slasher in the '80s. The horror movie gained a cult following for its outlandish deaths. The town accommodated fans of the film with a tiny museum and tours of major landmarks in the movie: the diner, the gas station, the road on the way to the camp, the entrance to the camp—but never the camp, which was privately owned. Growing up in a town where tourists visited to commemorate the gruesome deaths of forgettable actors did not instill in Eli a desire to achieve or accomplish. He lived without ambitions the way slugs live without shells. When it came time to apply for colleges, he applied to only the most mediocre institutions that America offered, the institutions where his friends were applying, and because he was not a bad student—although not a student worthy of praise—he was admitted to all of them. He chose a school in the desert known for its parties. If someone had listed the schools that admitted Elizabeth—Pomona and Vassar and Hinneman and Dartmouth and Amherst and Pratt—he would've guessed these were names of catalog sweaters or generals from fledgling American wars. She accepted a full-ride at Hinneman, the number-three-ranked college in the nation, according to *US News and World Report*, whereas Eli's school bounced around the two hundreds, he would have discovered, if he ever bothered to look.

They came from different places and went to different places. They were on safely separate trajectories. They were never meant to meet each other. Surely they were not destined for love, someone would think—if that someone pored over their lives. But no one, that same someone should know, is ever *meant* for anyone else. No life is ever even the skinniest bit of predictable. People collide. They bounce away after collisions, or veer away to avoid those collisions, creating lives accidentally. Circumstances pinball people together. This is called fate because *chance* is too scary a word. People collide. People collide. Elizabeth and Elijah were people. No better than anyone else. Fortunately, no worse.

**M**iss Valerie and I said nothing on the drive back to my apartment. I kept waiting for the walls of this hallucination to crumble, for the hands attached to my wrists to thicken and the splashes of pink polish on my nails to dissolve. Any minute, I believed, I would wake up gasping in a cold sweat on the couch, my body my own, but I remained severely buckled into this world—and into Elizabeth's skin—as Miss Valerie veered her steely hatchback through the slender Bulgarian streets.

"Call me in the morning," she said, as we idled in front of my building. I detected a deep sense of compassion for what she believed had befallen me—that my husband had abandoned our marriage, that it had caused me to unravel. I got out of the car without saying goodbye.

The building's front door was heavier than I remembered, and I needed to squat slightly for leverage and pull with both hands to open it. I tried taking the steps two at a time, but my toes only stretched as far as the corner of the second step. Elizabeth was six inches shorter than I was, and she found this habit of mine frustrating and selfish. "Are you trying to run away from me?" she would holler, a full flight below me as we trudged up to our apartment. I never slowed down for her. Not until now, when I had no other choice.

The apartment was how I had left it only a few hours earlier. In the back corner, far from the entrance, was the twin bed that came with the space. It was too small for two people to share, and I slept on a firm orange sectional facing the balcony. I had experience accepting whatever was given to me. The bed was made, a single pillow flat at the base of the headboard. Beside the bed the bureau doors were ajar. Elizabeth's dresses and my button-down shirts were bunched together on a hanger rod meant for one person's clothes. My blanket was folded loosely on the couch, which faced the glass sliding door that led onto the balcony, and on the balcony were clothes I had hung out to dry shortly after the thunderstorm ended this morning. My laptop sat beneath a pile of books on top of what I used as a desk: a rickety TV tray we had found folded flat under the couch.

Elizabeth worked at an actual desk, albeit a small one, hardly any wider than her shoulders, but it was a new desk, bought at a furniture warehouse on the outskirts of town. The fellowship paid very little, and we did not have enough money to purchase two desks. I didn't resent Elizabeth for the desk. She was the more accomplished writer between us. She had a graduate degree. Her writing had appeared in major magazines. Literary agents emailed her every few weeks, asking whether she had a completed novel, and, when she told them she hadn't, they asked her to please please *pleeeeease* send it to them once it was finished. Every morning she worked on her novel at the superior desk. I accepted this arrangement as a necessary sacrifice that enabled me to live abroad without working, my only requirements consisting of cooking and cleaning and writing and sex on the occasions when both of us were in the mood.

I was not a talentless writer. However, my writing lacked honesty and courage, the very things I most admired about Elizabeth's fiction, her impulse to dive into herself like a free-jumper leaving a cliff. She pulled from our everyday lives to create her fiction, and it wasn't uncommon to see arguments we'd had in our kitchen reappear in the stories she published, the details massaged, the stakes quietly raised, our barbs sharpened for greater effect, the differences so slight that I frequently accepted her fictions as truth and, often, after reading multiple drafts, would feel shame over the things the character based on me said to the character based on her. I would apologize, to which she would laugh and say, "Oh, I made that one up."

Though I had published a few stories in defunct online magazines, I was not, by any definition, a professional writer—I was a bartender and a server and had been since I was fourteen, when I got my first job slicing pizzas. My writing was fantastical and glumly humorous, like an old sock with a smiley face drawn on the toe. It was marked by avoidance and artifice. I feared looking inward. Writing was where I went to get away from myself, whereas Elizabeth wrote to understand herself and the human condition. Her talent was larger than mine, and I was grateful—so very grateful, I often reminded myself—that love had carved me a key to her life. Even my name, Eli, fit neatly at the front of hers, like a single step leading into a library. I was lucky. I had everything that I needed. So what if I worked on a TV tray? Elizabeth wrote literature with a capital *L*. She deserved a desk with a capital *D*.

I spent the day hunting through the apartment for some tuggable thread that might loosen this fantasy. Perhaps Elizabeth had left a note for me in the cupboard, or beneath the mattress, or behind the single framed print of Matisse's *Red Studio*—which she had hung in her bedrooms since childhood. But I found nothing. And I ended the search frustrated by the unfamiliar dimensions of Elizabeth's body. I now needed to stand on the stool she used to reach the top shelves in the cabinets; I needed both hands to upend the mattress; my arms, comparatively hairless, seemed slippery when I grazed my skin; I removed Elizabeth's bra eagerly and not without guilt for having never known this feeling, the freedom she sought at the end of long days. What is a body but limits? After twenty-eight years, I'd grown accustomed to my personal limits, the places I couldn't fit, the clothes I could no longer wear, the objects I could carry and for how long, the cans I could retrieve in supermarkets from unobtainable shelves—I stood a sliver under six feet—and, for the time being, all that knowledge I'd gathered was as useless as a rumor I couldn't confirm.

I remained in front of the mirror as night washed off the day. In our bathroom—where the showerhead hovered over the toilet, the toilet scrunched next to the sink—I studied Elizabeth's face as if I might will it back into my own. Before leaving the States, she had cut her hair into a severe bob she found unnatural—so unlike the wavy, marker-black hair she kept through our first three years of dating—but so close to her, I found it suited her better than long hair ever had; it fit snugly against her cheekbones, her skin pale and artful inside the frame of the bob. I'd been buzzing my hair for years, out of convenience and economy, and I enjoyed the novelty of tucking hair behind my ears and letting it flop free.

I smiled repeatedly, impressed by her teeth, so loudly white compared with the dull, coffee-stained yellow of mine. She was beautiful in an exacting way, the way a sketch could be beautiful. Her neck was generous, thin, her breasts small—the size I preferred—her nose tilted slightly upward, eyes seaglass green. Her brows were wide and dark; slashed through the center of one was a scar from a dog bite she'd received as a girl, a bite that very well could've killed her had it landed somewhere more tender. If I had been asked to remark on these attributes a week earlier, if, say, Elizabeth had gone missing—her in her body that is—and I had to file a police report, or describe her face to a sketch artist, I would not have been able to rattle off many of these features. Did I know her eye color? Did I know that her earlobes were attached? Of course, on some level I did, because I recognized her, every morning I would see her, in the kitchen or bed, and without thinking I would accept that yes, this was her, this was my partner—but I don't think I had ever effectively studied her like I did then, and I found the act unnerving and erotic. She was entirely new and alien to me.

There were other things that I could have done, other

experiments and boundaries to test, all the fun stuff from TV shows and movies where people swap bodies. As a child, I watched a short-lived sitcom about a pair of men who live with a woman above a pizza parlor. The sitcom lasted two seasons, at most, and the only episode I remember is a Halloween special where the hornier of the two men trades bodies with the woman. His first impulse, as her, is to enter the bathroom and ogle her breasts—which were suddenly his. He is not shown in the bathroom, but after he exits the woman, as him, chastises him, as her, and the laugh track cascades while he, as her, knowingly eyes the camera. Even as a child, I considered it a lurid display of manhood. The guy grossed me out. His actions were so puerile and predictable; they drew a fence around what I allowed myself in this new body.

I did not call my mother or Elizabeth's parents. What could I tell them? That I had become Elizabeth? Her mother was a therapist—she would have me committed if I said such a thing. I needed to learn more about what had happened before I went to them. I waited for some sign of Elizabeth to appear, for her voice, as if emerging from a swallowed locket, to speak over mine, but nothing of her existed inside me, there were only my recognizable thoughts.

Eventually, I realized that my phone was not in the apartment. I assumed it must be with Elizabeth, whom I assumed was inside my body, which, I hoped, was dressed in my clothes, or anyone's clothes, or at the very least—or very best—enjoyably nude. I called myself using Elizabeth's phone, but after ten or so tries the calls rushed ringless to voicemail, either a sign the phone had died or that she had blocked her number. According to an explainer online—which included advice to "take a hint"—it was impossible to distinguish a dead battery from a block without resorting to extrajudicial measures.

I tried to will myself to sleep with two full doses of Nyquil and one melatonin. I didn't want to sleep—the smart thing seemed to be to stay up all night, ready for a message from Elizabeth—but I wanted to believe that sleep might set everything right. I even settled onto the couch, where *I* normally slept, to create perfect conditions for returning to my own body.

But the sleep aids were not enough. And, deep in the night, I spied the uncanny singe of a cigarette glowing outside on the balcony. We shared the balcony with our neighbor, an aging Bulgarian woman we were told to call Vivien. She had lived in this building since it went up, and she liked to smoke late at night, at two or three in the morning. Her smoking disturbed Elizabeth. Less her smoking, that is, than where she chose to do it: on the balcony Elizabeth considered *ours*. Vivien had a front balcony, too, whereas we only had access to the balcony connected to her apartment, and though Vivien shared the balcony with every past fellow who lived in this studio, Elizabeth felt uneasy about a neighbor seeing into our living room.

I didn't see the big deal. I never saw the big deal.

"What if we're having sex?" she said.

"I doubt she'd watch us having sex."

"But she *could*," Elizabeth said. True. Technically, Vivien *could*, and though I doubted she would, I didn't say this to Elizabeth. Marriage had taught me to keep things to myself. I could not say, for instance, that I felt we had no right to prevent her from using the balcony—it had been hers for years before we arrived—because the situation disturbed Elizabeth, so it had to disturb me as well. And, when she asked Miss Valerie to talk to our landlord, who would in turn talk to Vivien, I supported her, as a good husband must, and when Vivien continued using the balcony, I helped Elizabeth draft an email to Miss Valerie making clear why we needed the balcony to ourselves, and when she informed us that the landlord informed her that she'd spoken to Vivien, I commiserated with Elizabeth when we woke one morning to find cigarette butts on the balcony, a sign Vivien had lied to the landlord, or the landlord had lied to Elizabeth's mentor, or Elizabeth's mentor had lied to us both. Or more likely: Vivien didn't care one bit about our request.

It was not the first time I'd noticed the glow of Vivien's cigarette burning in the dark. But for every time her smoking roused me from sleep, it woke Elizabeth three times. In the mornings, Elizabeth and I would fight over my apathy. I was supposed to defend her. Vivien's actions were an affront to us both, a threatening display of control, and my failure to shoo her away indicated I didn't care about Elizabeth, or myself, or our marriage. It was proof of my cowardice. Rather than cowardice, though, I considered myself driven by a desire for peace. Most nights I only wanted to get back to sleep. A woman smoking on her balcony wasn't a problem for me to solve. I would clench my eyes and spin away from the window, my face pressed into the couch cushions, waiting to hear Vivien's door sliding open and shut.

Tonight, however, I didn't turn away from the window. Sleepless, I felt righteously livid and unreasonable, as if Vivien had gotten me into this mess with her smoking. Deblanketed, I stomped to the door and pounded on the glass. Vivien peered at me, mid-cigarette, the orange ash curling down like a sigh. "Go inside!" I shouted. "This is my balcony."

Even in the dark, I detected her amusement. She put up her hand in a gesture of de-escalation and, before turning toward her apartment, she nodded at me and made an OK sign with her left hand. She laughed loudly enough to hear through the glass.

Laughing at what, I wondered, but then I looked down. I fell asleep wearing aged mesh running shorts and a loose gray T-shirt. The shorts hung askew on my hips. Sometime in my sleep, I must have tugged off my T-shirt—I normally slept shirtless—and above the shorts, exposed for all of Bulgaria, were Elizabeth's flat stomach and small, bare breasts. I crossed my arms to cover myself and was struck by how unfamiliar it felt to hold Elizabeth as Elizabeth. Yesterday had not been a nightmare. Elizabeth's body was mine. Shame warmed me like a fever. I returned to bed—the twin bed—and, after I tossed for a few hours, sunlight crept through the window.

arling," Elizabeth's mother said when I answered the phone. "How are you coping today?" Four days had passed since The Incident (as I was now calling it). Like everyone else, Johanna assumed that I was grieving the inexplicable disappearance of my husband. I had made little attempt to dispel her of this notion. It was easier to let her conclusions shape my actions, and it allowed me to say little in conversation. I spoke in Elizabeth's voice, miles higher than mine, but stripped of her conviction and confidence and the phrases she loved. I worried that saying too much might give me away, that soon some childhood New Jersey idiom would spring out like a bird from a cage, alerting Johanna.

She put me on edge in even the most mundane situations. She spoke with a destabilizing impatience that made me feel like a glass globe being tossed carelessly between her hands. She was not the type of person you aimed to impress; she was the type you hoped would leave you unscathed. She would see through my flawed mannerisms and tics if she visited. I wasn't ready for that kind of scrutiny. So I absorbed the story she told me: Eli had disappeared. He had abandoned me in Bulgaria without warning. I was devastated.

Johanna had been calling from Elizabeth's childhood home in Michigan at least three times every day since The Incident, calls in the morning, the afternoon, and the evening, time differences be damned, while emailing and texting to keep me company. I appreciated the gesture. Without Elizabeth, I longed for companionship, for the physical touches and habits and sounds that make up a life with someone—the gestures and murmurs and glances that were especially important here, isolated from friends and family and entrusted only to each other all day every day. Johanna's check-ins offered a welcome reprieve from my loneliness.

She treated my grief with professional respect and caution. She spoke tactfully about her absent son-in-law. She did not like to apologize. Elizabeth made this clear to me, early in our relationship, after she and her mother argued over a point where Johanna was clearly mistaken. I suspect that she spoke with such tact because she didn't want to say something she knew she could never—and would never—walk back.

"Fear manifests in a terrible way for some men," she reassured me this morning. "We both know the childhood Eli had—how things were with his parents. That doesn't excuse anything. Don't think that I'm taking his side over yours. He ought to feel terrible for how he treated you—no respect whatsoever. But even as you hold him accountable, acknowledge his terror. People don't do what he did unless they are terrified."

"Why are you defending him?" I asked. I was genuinely

curious. It didn't make sense for her to sympathize with the man who'd abandoned her daughter.

"Do you remember going to Disney World for your brother's soccer tournaments?"

"Vaguely," I lied.

"We never went to Disney itself. We weren't that type of family. You know that. Just the thought of it." She laughed with a snort of distaste. I loved her laugh, always so arrogant and correct. "But your brother and father were in the sports complex all day for three days. You must've been eleven or twelve. The organization running the tournament tried to make the complex amenable to the children who weren't playing. It was a massive bubble of soccer fields, eight, ten fields, maybe more, packed together like plaid. There were hordes of brothers—older and younger—scrambling over the grounds, their mouths popsicle red, fingers sticky as glue, all looking to run off their boredom.

"You, however, mostly read on the sidelines. You had no right to be as patient as you were during that trip, a wasted three days of your summer. I feel bad for taking you there, but we had no other choice. You know that. We couldn't leave you alone at the house. But you seemed unbothered—or you put up with it, I don't know. I appreciate it, I'm trying to say."

"It's fine," I said. Elizabeth would've been fuming. The attention her parents lavished on her brother, despite his pedestrian accolades—compared to hers—had dug at her since childhood.

"One day, while your brother was practicing, you and I explored the grounds outside the complex. There were baseball fields, and on one of them the tournament organizers set up a competition for the kids who weren't playing soccer. The goal was to hit a home run. It was a small field—from what I could tell—but still, it's quite the task for a child. They promised a gift certificate to Foot Locker for the winner, a hundred dollars or something. And you, you saw those other boys swinging away, repeatedly missing or slapping the ball right into the dirt, none of them even reaching the outfield, and you asked me—no, you *told* me to sign you up. You were that way from the beginning. When you saw an opportunity to succeed, you took it. You knew how great you were—you were ruthless about it. That's what I most admire in you. You never look back. You commit to be great and become even better. Me? I always look back. I am a pillar of salt."

It surprised me to hear her say that—I never saw her as a person shaped by regrets. "Do you really mean that?" I asked, thinking I might reassure her.

"I knew better than to talk you out of joining the competition," she said. "But the guy running it, some squat furry man, like one of those Star Wars bears—I swear you were taller than him at eleven—he looks up at you and says, 'Are you sure, sweetie?' You didn't respond. You gave him your name to put on his list. One by one the boys took their five little swings to hit a home run. There's a long line ahead of you. Twenty or so boys, with you at the end. So many boys, recklessly confident, strutting right to the plate, missed all five swings. The boy right before you swung so hard he fell on his bottom. It was pitiful. Truly. And the ones who *did* make contact, they were lucky if the ball rolled out of the infield. Nonetheless, you stayed in the line, stretching your arms in big circular motions, twisting your trunk back and forth—I have no idea where you learned those moves—and when it was your turn, the furry man, he again asked if you really wanted to, and again you didn't say anything. You nodded. He handed over the bat and gave a thumbs-up to the man tossing the balls.

"I know you're *sooooo tired of hearing this*," she said, poorly imitating her daughter.

"I don't mind," I said. I was surprised Elizabeth never told me this story—early in our relationship, she would hold me rapt for hours in bed, tracing the arc of her life across my bare stomach, creating a personal mythology of triumphs and lovers and friends and ambitions and even the occasional shame. She wanted me to know everything. But not, apparently, this.

"Because it's different this time," Johanna said. "Stories are always changing—you understand this better than anyone—or what I mean is we're changing, even when the story remains the same. We change and thus we change the story, to better fit the person we are. I bet you could finish it for me, in your own way, of course. You know what happens next and I know you don't believe me—but I swear to you, Lizzy, I swear you would've hit that ball ten thousand feet. I would not be surprised if the ball is still in the air, floating in space. You should've *seen* the look on the other boys' faces. All of them, every last boy on that field, erupted in tears, waterworks, a flooding hazard, as the ball sailed over the fence."

I laughed. "There's no way all the boys started crying."

"Your first try, too! You didn't need five swings—not even close. And their parents," she said. "My god. Boys and their dads weeping uncontrollably. Children and parents consoling each other. I'd never seen anything like it—and they, the parents, the boys, they clearly had never seen anything like it. Like you. You placed the bat silently on home plate and returned to me without the slightest celebration. Not even a fist pump—your father was like that too, when he swam. No emotion at all. I handed over your book and approached the organizer to ask for your prize. The Foot Locker—or someplace, I don't know, some sporting goods store in the area. It was part of the deal. It was the only reason you tried, I thought. So I asked the guy where we could pick up the prize. And no shame at all, this man tells me he can't possibly give you the gift certificate. He tells me the boys are shaken. They're hurt. They're embarrassed. I don't know what word he used but it was one of those. Like I said: pitiful. And when I returned to you, to tell you he couldn't give you the prize—the hundred dollars you earned—you said, 'I know,' like you'd expected that from the beginning, or like you could sense that you'd created a problem by hitting the ball, by doing what those boys couldn't. Does that make sense?"

It made sense, but I wasn't sure why she was telling Elizabeth this story today.

"Those boys on the field," she said, "those boys are now men. They're men like Eli—I hate to say it. I assumed he was better than them, I really did have faith, and perhaps he'll prove me wrong. But I doubt it. Boys become men who are ill-equipped for women's accomplishments. Women do something they can't and they weep, or they disappear."

"You think Eli ran away because of the fellowship?" Did she really think I was so fragile?

"You're both so young—god, twenty-eight. You're children! And men's brains, I'm not sure if you know, but they don't fully develop until they're thirty. That on top of all the conditioning, all the trauma."

"Eli isn't like that," I said. "He's very mature."

"Of course I'm furious at him. I plan to tell him when he returns—and it seems obvious to me, from my vantage point, all the people I've seen over the years, that he will return. I won't blame you if you don't take him back. I wouldn't. But don't cast him as a villain. Not yet, at least. Nothing good comes from prematurely casting someone as a villain. You're a writer—people are far more complicated than what they have done. You know this. You wouldn't be so talented if you didn't."

For years, Elizabeth sensed in her mother a tangled thread of envy over her writing achievements. Her parents had stopped producing work shortly before Elizabeth was born. She considered herself the reason they hadn't continued pursuing the arts. The feeling I got on the phone, though, was a genuine wellspring of pride and affection flowing from mother to daughter. Elizabeth felt guilty for pursuing the life that her parents once aspired to live. This guilt had created a rift between them, or so Elizabeth thought, and her mother's tenderness saddened me. I missed Elizabeth more, then, than I had over the previous days; I wanted her to know how her mother truly felt. Johanna's admiration was wasted on me.

"I doubt this makes you feel better," she said.

"It does," I told her.

Johanna told me she loved me and promised to call later that evening with Henry, Elizabeth's father. I carried her promise with me through the day like an egg that might hatch in my hand.

Talking to my own mother proved far more complicated. In normal times, she and I did not have a strong relationship. We were at our closest when separated by thousands of miles. Distance freed us from the intimacy expected of mother and son. Even when I was a teenager, we'd had trouble living together, and as an adult venturing home for the holidays, I rarely spent time in the same room with her, except for the obligatory unwrapping of presents. Throughout my stay, we would drift past each other in the halls en route to separate rooms, waving and nodding, like colleagues hired into the same family.

Living abroad had strengthened our relationship. Over my first few months in the country, she texted me most afternoons—Bulgarian time—upon waking up back in New Jersey. For the first time in my life, I knew her routines. I knew, for instance, that on Tuesdays she went out for clams with friends and that on Fridays she met up with different friends at a different pub, where they would commandeer the juke-box and sing until the bar emptied. I knew about the tricks she was teaching her puppy, a black lab named Grover, who, days before The Incident, she had taught to hold up his paw in exchange for a treat. She delivered lunches to homebound elderly women on Mondays. I liked viewing her life at a remove. From this vantage, she existed inside a fantasy of satisfaction I created for her. She had a routine; she was happy; probably happy.

I wasn't so naive to think she had fundamentally changed since I moved to Bulgaria. But living so far from her distress lightened my emotional burden. She was an adult. I couldn't help her to work through whatever grief I sensed in her life. Instead, we focused on the positive. I told her about the cats in the streets—before getting Grover, she'd only housed cats, sometimes up to six at a time. I sent her photos of Elizabeth and me posing foolishly at the foot of the town's towering statue of the Madonna. I described in elaborate detail the tomato-based traditional Bulgarian meals and ranked the local spirits, promised to send her a bottle of my favorite rakia. And, for the first time in my life, I spoke to her honestly about my writing anxiety, how scared I was to pursue this career and how small I felt in the shadow of Elizabeth's talent—perhaps Johanna was right about me, that I was the type of man who couldn't handle a woman's success. My mom and I reached a level of intimacy neither of us had thought possible before I left the US. And for this reason—along with the obvious reason—she took Eli's disappearance especially hard.

She and I spoke after my call with Johanna. "Lizzy," she

said. "How could Eli do this to you? It isn't like him to do this to you. Or to me. You're sure he didn't say anything?"

Whatever connection we'd built, over my first few months abroad, had become irretrievable once I'd migrated to Elizabeth's body. I didn't have the energy to explain this to her. If I told her the truth, she would ask questions that I did not know how to answer, and her hypothetical interrogation, contrived in my mind, made me feel bratty and resistant. Even as Elizabeth, my impulse was to hide myself from my mother.

"Eli always kept so much to himself," I said.

"Not recently, though," she said. Tears softened her words. "You probably don't know this, but our relationship had never been better. We were finally talking, like mother and son. He was telling me everything."

"He mentioned this."

"There are things you keep from your wife. I'm sorry. It's true. That's just how marriages are. Men keep things from their wives, women keep things from their husbands. But you don't keep things from your mother."

Her territorial grief filled me with pity. But her arrogance angered me. We weren't *that* type of mother and son, even if we had grown closer, and I didn't like her pushing this narrative onto Elizabeth and, most likely, countless other friends. There was so much I would never tell her. I told her I needed to go. If I stayed on the line, I would say something hurtful.

"Don't be offended, Lizzy," she said. "You take offense to every little thing and we don't have time for that now."

"Is that what Eli said about me?" I couldn't remember whether I had, and I hated the idea of having been so dismissive, because I knew it wasn't unlike me.

"My child is missing," she said.

"Call me tomorrow," I said.

"My only child."

I hung up the phone.

**Y**ou can't obsess over things," Kiril said. "It doesn't make sense that he left but it happened. That's what you have to accept." Kiril was a slim and voluble man who wore wire-framed glasses and kept his black beard neatly trimmed. He dressed conventionally. For him, clothes were merely a necessity, and today, in the café he owned with his fiancée, Desi, he wore his pouchy white smock and jeans.

Desi stood behind the counter ringing up a woman for two coffees. I was sitting on a floral couch in the corner of the room, beneath a wall-mounted flat-screen TV that was playing the news. I was self-conscious about how I positioned my body. Elizabeth normally had wonderful posture, and when I first sat down, I kept my back eager and upright, though it soon occurred to me that, in her grief, she would have had every reason to slouch. I slumped my shoulders an inch, no more, a compromise between routine and despair.

Six days had passed since The Incident, and today was my first time leaving the apartment to see other people. I'd gone on brief walks to experiment with Elizabeth's gait but had avoided everyone who might recognize me, chiefly Desi and Kiril, our only real friends in the city. Elizabeth still had not contacted me. This was the longest we'd been apart in nearly a year, and our first separation since we moved to Bulgaria—other than Elizabeth's time at the school. All week I kept waiting for her to appear behind me in the apartment, for the past six days to reveal themselves as a dream, or like a thief removing his mask. I was grieving without being sure what to grieve. I had lost Elizabeth even as I'd retained her. It wasn't her body that I missed, because now I had an even more intimate relationship to her body, but I didn't not miss her body—I longed for the peculiar ways Elizabeth carried her body, for the feeling of looking up to see her across the room, knowing she was separate but with me. I missed her mind, her winks and sly jokes, the way she crumpled over her desk in exhaustion after a long day of writing, how I would come to her, curl her upright, and kiss her on the forehead and tell her I loved her. I missed the rare tanginess under her arms after a run. I missed how her eyes grew moony when we imagined the future together, a house in the woods with walls full of books and a dining room where we hosted friends every weekend. It never occurred to me how much went into a person, how I could both be Elizabeth and feel completely apart from her.

As desperate as I was for Elizabeth, and for all this to go back to normal, I was just as desperate to see other people and hold conversations that weren't with parents over the phone. Kiril's lecture didn't bother me. I welcomed the communication, feigning gratitude for his unsolicited wisdom. Elizabeth found this tendency in him aggravating; his lectures, according to her, were predictably informed by sex. I had never been lectured at. To me, Kiril's sexism—though that sounds too harsh for what I am describing—seemed like the ingrained habit of someone who truly meant well. English was, after all, his second language, and we couldn't judge him for failing to display the nuance of lifelong English speakers. My excuses taxed Elizabeth's patience. After returning home from evenings with Kiril and Desi, she would mime drawing a curtain around the twin bed to indicate she needed privacy for the rest of the night.

"If he doesn't come back, then it's his loss," Kiril said. "He is a fool to give up on you and your marriage. Family is what life is about. He is crazy to give it away."

Unlike Elizabeth, I didn't mind being pitied. This sympathy of strangers and friends gave me a sense of purpose. What pity stripped of my autonomy it made up for in attention directed at me; I valued attention more than I valued my dignity.

Kiril made an expression to summon Desi over. My confusion and pain made him uncomfortable. Like a lot of men, he took pride in his ability to fix things; he believed reason could extinguish emotional woe, and, faced with a problem he couldn't reason away, he passed me over to Desi.

She took a stiff seat on the couch beside me and left a wide space between us. Desi was taller than Kiril, unnoticeably so, and she kept her straight blond hair pulled back in a ponytail, always, the end resting along on her spine. Her nose and mouth were small, but her eyes were large, intentionally so, I sometimes felt, as if she had trained herself to observe instead of consume. Traces of flour dusted her collarbones and collected in the folds of her knuckles. She disliked working here—the café had been Kiril's idea—and, despite constantly washing her hands, she never seemed to soap off all the flour.

Elizabeth's work schedule prevented her from building the same closeness I had established with Desi and Kiril. I often stopped in to see them before walking to Elizabeth's school. I would pop in the café and ask how business was going, trade a few leva for a scone, and eat it on the way to school. Our four-person friendship was built on these brief interactions. It would not have been unusual for Desi to drape her arm over *my* shoulder, to console me if Elizabeth left, but she had trouble doing the same for the woman sitting beside her—and I ached for both Elizabeth and myself in that moment. After nearly a week on my own, I longed to be touched, in even the most innocuous or consoling way.

"There will be better days," Desi said. She inched closer and lowered her hands to my hands, where they rested on my knees, but after a gentle clasp—which caused me to tense up—she returned them to her lap.

Desi was older than Kiril by five years, thirty-six to his thirty-one—unimaginable ages from the safety of twenty-eight—and she saw life through a fogged windowpane of preemptive grief. They had met eight years earlier at a conservatory housed in a small Tennessee college. The conservatory catered exclusively to international students, and, because one of the instructors was Bulgarian, the greatest share of the student population came from Bulgaria. Desi arrived in Tennessee at twenty-eight in the aftermath of four troubling years playing piano for Saudi princes at a hotel in Riyadh. She didn't like to speak of her time as a performer, and, on the rare occasions she did, she spread scant crumbs of trauma, blinking details about men following her to the room she shared with six other performers or the manager who, nearly a decade later, still owed her a year's worth of paychecks.

She desperately wanted a child, and to be married, but Kiril insisted they needed to wait until they were financially independent. They shared an apartment with Kiril's parents. It didn't make sense to get married and have children while still living like children, he reasoned. Desi accepted this arrangement like a plant that had settled for shade.

She longed for marriage and children, Elizabeth gathered—she loved proposing theories about people who crossed through her life—not out of some girlhood fantasy but in reaction to years of instability. She gave off a sense of exhausted urgency. Some part of her seemed to have already accepted that the promises Kiril made to her wouldn't be kept. As soon as they could afford their own place, a new impediment would arise; Kiril would insist on buying a dog to better prepare them for children, to see if they truly had time to care for another life, and when he finally agreed that they were ready—fiscally, emotionally—her age would result in trouble conceiving. As she rounded into her forties, and as setbacks continued to mount, it would become obvious they had waited too long to conceive, and he would tell her that he cared about her too much to continue trying, because at her age it was a risk not only to their future child but to her. He didn't want to lose her, he would say, and when she conceded that he was right, that having a child was no longer a viable option, she would push to get married—for they still will not have been married—and Kiril would begin to wonder out loud whether they ought to even get married, since the point of marriage, after all, was to start a family. Wasn't that what they'd agreed on from the beginning? That marriage was, for them, the first step to building a family? It would be tragic, what had happened to them, and Kiril would always love Desi, but he wanted a family—she'd known that about him. He'd been saying for *years* that he wanted a family and a wife and, unfortunately, it appeared they couldn't have that life together, and if they couldn't build a family, then it was only right for them to separate. Kiril would be sorry. It would hurt him immensely to leave. But in the long run, it would be better for both of them.

According to Elizabeth, Desi lived two places at once: inside of her ongoing hope for the stability and inside the grief she knew to expect. When she lowered her hands to mine, the current of these conflicting feelings wriggled through me like static shock. "There will be better days." A sentence spoken to both of us.

"What makes you think that?" I asked.

"They have to get better," she said. "Or else they'll get worse."

I laughed, though I doubt that she had intended to make a joke. She tilted away from me, hurt by my reaction.

Kiril finished with a customer and pulled up a chair across from the couch. He asked when I would return to teaching.

"They gave me a week," I said. "I might take another week off."

"It sounds like you're quitting," he said.

"I can't quit."

"You should quit," Kiril said. "You have no reason to stay here."

"You can go see your family," Desi said.

"It's good to be with your people," Kiril said.

"They're loving parents," I said, because I wanted to say something that didn't mean anything. "I really miss them," I added, because Elizabeth missed them immensely, even before The Incident.

Desi tightened herself against me and lowered her head to my shoulder, a display of intimacy I didn't feel I had earned. In that instant, I knew she was the only person who would understand if I told her the truth. I didn't intend to tell her. Not her or anyone else. But Desi wouldn't doubt what I told her. She was capable of absorbing unbelievable truths.

"You don't have plans tonight?" Kiril asked.

"Don't tease her," said Desi.

He responded to her in Bulgarian and she shook her head, though I couldn't tell whether she was agreeing with him or showing disapproval.

"Eliz—" I started, then recovered to say, "Eli and I normally went out on Wednesday nights. We liked to split up the week with something exciting." The mistake went unnoticed—a benefit of such similar names.

"I know a great place," Kiril said. "I've been wanting to take you there since you arrived. Every Wednesday I would tell Desi to remind me to invite Eli when he came in the café, but every time she would forget."

She clicked her tongue at him. They passed more words in Bulgarian. Kiril waved his hand through the air, dismissing her.

"If you don't have plans we should go there tonight. They have the best fish in the city."

"I don't eat meat," I said, then tensed, realizing my mistake.

"You don't eat meat either?" Desi asked.

"That's what I mean," I said. "I so rarely ate meat around Eli." Desi bought it but with a look of suspicion.

"You need a night out," Kiril said. He shimmied his shoulders foolishly. "You need to take your mind off everything."

The last few nights alone in the studio had been miserable. "I'll think about it," I told them, and stood up, gathered my things.

"Be back here at seven," Kiril said. "And wear something nice."

Desi chided him in Bulgarian and slapped his forearm. He flashed an impish smile.

"This place is nothing special," she said.

"We'll find you a nice Bulgarian man," Kiril said.

"Maybe," I said, as I slipped out the front door.

I HADN'T DRESSED MYSELF DELIBERATELY SINCE ELIZABETH disappeared. Over the last few days on my own, I'd traded off between sweatpants and shorts, layering myself under generations of hoodies. Visiting the café was my first venture out of the studio, and I had been lucky to escape that conversation without them remarking on my negligent outfit or the unwashed sheen of my hair.

They would have understood if I declined their invitation. Desi would have understood. But I couldn't spend every night in the studio. Vivien had taken to smoking even more often on our shared balcony, undeterred by my outburst. Her presence didn't seem threatening. But there's a moment right before threatening when it's hard to discern whether someone is a danger to you or if it's all in your head, and that was where Vivien now resided.

This wasn't the type of activity Elizabeth normally attended. Had Kiril invited us out, two weeks earlier, she would have stayed home to write while I joined them alone, as if I were scouting the world for safety. I liked the idea of doing something Elizabeth wouldn't. If I were going to be her, then I may as well be her on my terms. I occupied a space where neither she nor I seemed to exist, free from the expectations of our personalities.

Though Desi warned me against dressing fancy, I wanted to try looking good, if nothing more than an exercise in this new body.

I had not, for instance, masturbated as her, though I was curious how it might feel, and I had confidence I might be successful—an ex had once referred to me as The King of Fingering, months after we broke up. But I couldn't shake the feeling that it would be disrespectful to objectify Elizabeth from inside her own body. Did I need her permission to finger her as her? I had never asked her permission to jack off, in my own body. Perhaps I hesitated now because I believed the arrangement was temporary. I had only showered once since The

Incident, and during that one time I scrubbed my body with the efficiency of a nurse before promptly leaving the bathroom. When I peed and shit, I wiped fastidiously, even wastefully, piling entire rolls in the bowl, intent on leaving Elizabeth's body as I had found it.

I was generally clumsy. I had broken many pieces of dishware that Elizabeth brought into the relationship; I dirtied an heirloom rug by entering the apartment still wearing running shoes; I crashed her bike the one time I rode it. Elizabeth had tensely forgiven me for these mistakes, but my clumsiness burdened her, and The Incident, at times, seemed like the ultimate test: Could I care for her properly while she was gone?

The best way to respect her, that evening, was to make her appear as beautiful as possible. Elizabeth didn't dress up very often, but on special occasions, she liked wearing a sleeveless burgundy wrap dress. It was classy and flattering without revealing too much, cut to the center of her breasts. I loved catching flashes of thigh when she crossed her legs. She looked beautiful in the dress. No, she looked hot. The dress turned me on, and she knew it. Sometimes she wore it to mundane outings—trips to get pizza, a night at the movies—to entice me into having sex when we returned home.

We didn't have sex as often as she liked, and her ability to predict my desires and needs embarrassed me. I did not like to be known. I preferred to be misunderstood and cryptic, like an inkblot or a footprint on a carpet. Dating for three years, living together for two, marriage—they all had made me obvious to her, and it was something I had to accept.

PEOPLE COLLIDE

In the dress, I understood why she wore it. I felt sexy and desired even before leaving the studio. I rarely felt this way in my own body—even on the occasions when Elizabeth told me she loved my physique. No compliment ever seemed real to me, especially from the people who loved me, people who, I believed, were obligated out of love to compliment me and thus had every reason to lie. Our loved ones love us too much to tell us the truth. Wearing Elizabeth's dress, I sensed how it felt to be wanted. I wanted her, and I understood, reluctantly, the man from the sitcom, his desire to ogle himself. I entered the sliver of the bathroom to take a stab at putting on makeup.

She owned only a few products, mascara, two tubes of lipstick, and organic liquid foundation a shade paler than her cheeks. I pumped the foundation onto two fingers and dragged it over my cheeks, rubbing it in like suntan lotion, but all the skin untouched by foundation glowed with discoloration. I wiped it off and searched for a makeup tutorial on my phone.

Elizabeth did not like me touching her face. As a teenager, she saw a dermatologist—a cruel and taxing man, in the story she told—who instilled in her a fear of fingertip oils with the bluster of a priest warning his congregation about the magnetism of Satan. Early in our relationship, I lowered my hand to her face during sex, but she brushed it aside immediately, and not without anger. "Never try that again," she had said, once we finished. Through three years, I hadn't, and lifting my hand to her face seemed like an enormous betrayal.

It took me a few tries to find an appropriate makeup tutorial. Most of the videos proposed complicated designs best

47

suited for nights at a club, wide pink washes of eye shadow and wings that Elizabeth never applied. Worse, the women applying their makeup worked quickly and assumed a basic level of mastery far beyond mine. I finally discovered a video called "Easy Everyday Makeup Tutorial (with a bit of glam)" by a makeup artist named Eman. The video opened with a still shot of her face fully made up, the title hovering over her features, before eerily shifting to video like a statue that had awoken. She welcomed me with a generic "Hi, guys!" and suggested reading the description below to see the products she used in the video. I opened the description. There were nearly two dozen products, a terrifying number compared with the amount that Elizabeth owned. Nonetheless, I continued watching.

After the introduction, Eman's face starkly reverted to its pre-makeup form, her black hair stringing wetly down to her neck. She lacked the chipper demeanor of the other artists I'd watched and moved swiftly, almost severely, through the routine. As I waited for her to apply one of the products that Elizabeth owned, I became aware of Eman's inconsistencies, the redness at the edge of her nostrils—which she concealed on her face—and the sleeplessness hinted under her eyes, soon also concealed.

Eman pumped two squirts of sheen liquid foundation into her palm and buffed it into her skin using a 42 Skunk brush, a name I was sure I'd misheard, until I checked the description. Elizabeth did not own a skunk brush. I buffed in the foundation using two fingers, making polite swirls where Eman advised. She moved on to powder, which she used to set the foundation. Elizabeth didn't own any powder. Or bronzer. Or blush. Or eye primer. Or brushes number 12, 22, 6, and 15. She did, however, have eye shadow—only one color, not the four shades that Eman applied—and, though I didn't have primer, I brushed the gentle golden color over my lids, dusting it on with a move that felt reckless. I shakily ran a brown eye pencil along the upper edge of my eye. Eman and I rolled mascara up our lashes. Like Eman, I didn't have time to attach falsies. We moved to the lip. Elizabeth owned two lip colors. Eman went with a nude, so I went with the lighter of Elizabeth's options, a rosy color called Fairest in the Land. The lipstick was chunky from underuse. Eman used a similar color but a brand of much higher quality—its case like a large golden bullet—which, when applied, made her lips appear pristine and pillowy. At the end of the video, Eman advised me to subscribe and, grateful, I liked and subscribed, sure I'd watch another one of her videos soon.

The sight of Elizabeth startled me. Not because I'd done a poor job applying her makeup. For a first try, I'd done fairly well. Elizabeth looked lovely. And I had, with Eman's assistance, highlighted her eyes and concealed her exhaustion. But the person looking back at me wasn't the woman I knew. I had created some other Elizabeth. Not a person she had been hiding from me but a person who didn't exist. She normally wore her hair in a messy bun, but every time I tried to put her hair up, strands would whisper down in front of my eyes, creating a maddening curtain. After a handful of failures, I tugged out the hair tie, content with wearing her hair down. Anyone who saw me would've taken me for Elizabeth testing out a new look. But in the mirror all I saw were the differences between my Elizabeth and hers.

"YOU OVERDRESSED," KIRIL SAID, WHEN I MET HIM AND DESI outside the café.

"You look wonderful," Desi said.

I thanked her. I'd added a pair of chunky black heels to the outfit. Elizabeth was about six inches shorter than I was, and the heels added only two inches. I was nervous about wearing them out, convinced I'd topple over while walking, but whatever risk I had assumed was worth climbing a little higher toward my natural height. And I was pleased to once again be taller than Kiril, though only by a few hairs.

He unlocked the front door and beckoned us inside. He disappeared into the kitchen without explaining anything.

"You don't have to do this," Desi said. "He thinks this is a special occasion. I told him that's not what this is but he wouldn't listen to me." She apologized.

Kiril returned holding an unmarked green glass bottle and three stubby cups. "This is my father's rakia," he said. He took a spot behind the register, as if he were bartending. "Last year's batch. He says it's the best batch in all of Bulgaria."

"Is it?" I asked.

"I will not speak ill of my father," Kiril said, and bobbed his head side to side with a laugh, the Bulgarian equivalent of a playful American shrug. He poured the rakia into the cups and passed them to Desi and me. He said something in Bulgarian as he lifted his cup, and Desi flashed him a discouraging look. I drank without clinking, upset he'd cut me out of the toast.

The liquor tasted like burning, and, though Kiril compared it to vodka, it didn't taste like vodka at all. I wiped my wrist across my mouth and a drag of pink smudged the back of my hand. "What did you say?" I asked Kiril. "In your toast?" I suspected it had been about me.

"Just an old proverb," said Desi.

Kiril repeated the phrase, in Bulgarian.

"It doesn't mean anything," she assured me.

Her reaction made me even more curious, and I pestered Kiril until he finally offered a loose translation. "It's something like, 'May you find the one you're looking for.'"

"That's a mean thing to say," I said. "Considering my situation." I would have never said anything like this had I been myself. But Elizabeth respected herself. She would not let a comment like that slide.

"It's a common phrase," Kiril said. But his tone was sheepish.

"Let's take one more," I said. I could feel the power in the room shifting in my direction and I wanted it to continue.

"We'll drink at the bar," he said.

"It'll save us the cost of a round," I replied.

Desi eyed me tensely, with either admiration or fear, I couldn't tell.

He poured Desi's drink, then mine. Before he could fill his cup I flattened my hand over it. "You have to drive," I said. I wanted him to know I could retaliate. This was something

Elizabeth would do, half out of anger, half out of jest, and I liked defending her honor.

Delighted, Desi lifted her glass to mine. "To overdressing," she said. We emptied our glasses. Kiril hurried us out of the café.

THE RESTAURANT SAT TWENTY MINUTES OUTSIDE TOWN IN the moon-shadow of a shuttered textile factory. A massive chute like an elephant trunk plunged down from a shattered third-story window. The windows around it were small toothy yawns of broken glass.

Kiril parked in a slender gravel lot stuffed with cars parked at difficult angles. A floodlight fanned out from over the top of a screen door leading into the kitchen. The door clacked open. A man in a soiled apron lugged an ungainly green garbage bag to the dumpster. When he opened the lid, the scent of garbage crashed against me like a wave. Kiril greeted the man warmly by name as he passed us on his way to the kitchen, but the man was too busy to talk.

"Is he one of the single men you were talking about?" I joked.

"Only the first," Kiril said.

"The better men are inside," Desi said. She pressed a hand to my back and guided me toward the entrance. Her touch made me feel loved and nervous. The greater our intimacy, the more likely I might mess up my impression of Elizabeth.

Desi and I cautioned over the dips in the gravel, giggling drunkenly at our clumsiness. Kiril walked a few paces ahead of us, unamused. By the time Desi and I made it inside, he was already planted at a table in the corner of the main dining room. He held a laminated menu in front of his face.

"What's his deal tonight?" I asked, as if I didn't already know.

Desi shook her head: *Don't waste any time worrying about him.*

The tables were packed together like cows and draped with blue plasticky tablecloths designed with maps of the Balkans. Cigarette smoke floated overhead like a genie. I found the scent pleasant and was reminded of visiting my grandparents' house as a boy, sitting on a stool in their kitchen as my grandmother fried hush puppies and smoked, ash flaking into the oil.

"Nice of you to join me," he said.

Desi sat beside him against the wall. I squeezed onto the opposite side, bumping the chair behind me as I pulled mine out, but the man didn't notice. I contorted myself quietly into my seat.

"I ordered us beers," Kiril said.

Desi scrunched her neck to plant an uncomfortable kiss on his cheek.

"Unless you two want to keep drinking rakia. If your plan is to"—he put on a deep southern drawl to finish his sentence in an American accent—"get fucked up." He laughed with genuine pleasure. The phrase seemed like an old friend to him, likely muttered by his American pals in Tennessee.

Desi whispered into his ear. He made a face of exaggerated innocence.

The waitress placed three large brown bottles on our table. They were double the size of the beers I normally had when I drank, but, looking around the room, it seemed they were the only size this restaurant served. Elizabeth rarely drank. When she did, she never drank beer. Gluten muddled her thoughts, and a single Corona could sentence her to a crumbling hangover. She learned about her sensitivities reading online health forums and blogs hosted by unlicensed nutritionists. Both of us were susceptible to the assertions of charlatans. Whereas I found comfort believing that complicated workout routines would grant me the cut delts and ridged forearms I so deeply desired—I am uncomfortably vain—Elizabeth found a home in websites loaded with provocative claims about coconut oil and phytochemicals and adipose lung. She hunted through articles for diet advice after every migraine or prolonged bout of stomach distress, reading the recommendations like a scholar decoding ancient languages, backtracking through meals, activities, feelings, sensations, and vibes in search of whatever caused her discomfort.

Elizabeth was cursed with a body that let everything in. One night, at a house party thrown by one of my co-workers in Arizona, she met a man freshly dumped by his fiancée, and after minutes talking to him she needed to leave. The stranger's grief, she told me later, had infiltrated her as if it were her own. Despite her love and admiration for visual art, she rarely spent more than an hour inside museums. The intensity of her feelings in front of certain paintings shook her to her core. I was never this type of person. The world bounced off me like rocks on cement, and I continued moving, unaware that collisions had even occurred. Living in Elizabeth's body had not made me permeable or excessively sensitive—or perhaps I wasn't sensitive enough to recognize that I had become excessively sensitive—and I accepted my large, garish beer knowing the risks but hoping I wouldn't suffer as Elizabeth might or that my suffering, should it arrive, would be worth having fun with Kiril and Desi.

The waitress stood at the head of our table tapping her pen on her notepad. Kiril gestured in a circular motion to order for all of us. The only word I recognized was *kartofi*—potatoes—though I couldn't tell how they'd be prepared.

The waitress nodded and left.

"I didn't get a chance to look at the menu," I said.

"They make the best fried fish in the city," Kiril said. "There's no reason to order anything else." His actions balanced tensely between hospitable and controlling, but there was no point in arguing with him, because no matter *how* I felt, he considered his choices hospitable. We tapped the necks of our bottles together and drank.

When the waitress delivered the potatoes—steamed and dressed lightly in vinegar, flaked with fresh thyme—I was already done with my first beer. Desi tried to keep up with me. Like Elizabeth, she rarely drank, and the beer sloshed at eye level inside her. This was my first time drinking since The Incident. It wasn't smart, but the rakia unlocked doors I wanted to enter.

Desi reached for the waitress's wrist. She ordered two more beers for us. "But you haven't even finished this one," Kiril said, in English, to wall the waitress off from our argument.

Desi chugged the remaining swallows and passed her empty bottle and mine to the waitress. "Is that better?" She and I shared a conspiratorial grin, then cracked into laughter. Kiril waved to the waitress and spoke hurriedly in Bulgarian. She nodded. He turned morosely toward the wall, muttering to himself. I thrived amid these kinds of divisions. I had grown up with divorced parents and was adept at picking sides out of self-interest. Kiril made it easy, that night, to form an alliance with Desi. The condescension Elizabeth described to me, over the past couple of months, seemed obvious now, and I was embarrassed for not seeing it earlier.

The waitress set a mountain of fried, finger-size fish in the center of the table. The creatures gleamed in their grease. The uneaten potatoes cooled grimly on Kiril's side of the table. She pulled two small beer bottles out of her apron pocket and pried off the caps, set them down before Desi and me. We hadn't ordered smaller beers.

"You changed our order," I said to Kiril, once the waitress left.

Desi pinched her hand shut in a silencing motion.

"Eat the fish before it gets cold," he said. He lifted a pair between his middle finger and thumb and swallowed them whole like a seal.

Desi sat upright with her arms crossed.

Kiril ate three more fish. He nodded at the plate. "They're terrible cold."

I ate a single fish, out of politeness, or boredom. It tasted like breading. Desi and I took long swigs in solidarity. Kiril nudged her elbow with his and spoke to her in Bulgarian. He nodded again at the fish. I ate another. Its bones crunched under my molars.

"This fish isn't good," Desi said, in English.

Kiril responded in Bulgarian.

"Just because it is the best in town does not mean it is good," she said.

He lifted one of the fish to her mouth as if feeding a child, but she swept his hand away and retightened her arms over her chest.

"This is old fish, Elizabeth," she said. "They fry it so you can't taste it's about to expire."

Kiril spoke quietly into her ear.

"I don't care," she said.

"This isn't the right time," he said in English. "We're having a wonderful night."

"In Riyadh," Desi said, "at the hotel where I used to perform, the chefs would treat us to a fancy hotel meal every Thursday. The hotel chefs were very talented. They were like me. They had been brought to Riyadh to perform for wealthy men in the city—and to be paid very little. The Thursday night meals were a perk written into our contracts. The chefs were told to prepare us the lowest-quality fancy meal they could provide. Simple pasta dishes or leftover soups, whatever could reasonably be considered a quality dinner. But one, the chef's assistant?"

"Sous chef," I said.

"Ramon," she said. "From Portugal. He liked me. He said I was very pretty—and he was handsome. The most handsome man in the hotel." She gave a girlish laugh. I'd never seen her so joyful.

"You are very beautiful," Kiril said, too late to stop her.

"Every Thursday night, when it was our night to eat at the restaurant, the other musicians would receive their simple, contractual meals whereas Ramon would prepare a single dinner especially for me, the finest dish of the night. Even the rich people at the hotel never ate as well as I did on Thursday nights. As the other musicians slurped their soup, or stabbed their forks into rice, I would saw through a buttery steak and lift asparagus to my mouth. Ramon made me feel that I deserved better than the other musicians. I was more talented than they were. Ramon, too, was more talented than everyone else in the kitchen, even the chef, but he worked at the hotel to pay for his brother's schooling. Their mother died when he was fourteen and his brother was six. Their father, a drunk, spent their savings on skunky red wine and football bets. His brother was a genius, Ramon insisted, and he couldn't let his genius go to waste. So he'd taken this job because it promised a salary without paying for housing or food. He sent every dollar he made to his brother, who wanted to go to college in the US. He was one of the few good people in that hotel. And I loved that this good person saw something good in me too.

"We only saw each other on Thursdays. And only late in the night, around two in the morning or three, once he finished deep cleaning the kitchen—a weekly task that always fell to him because the head chef resented his talent. I enjoyed the simple rhythms of our relationship. He prepared elaborate meals for me. We would meet in the garden behind the hotel, where I would sing for him—though my voice was the worst of my talents—and he would tell me he loved what I sang, and I never felt he was lying or flattering me, which is how I normally feel when men offered me praise." Desi adjusted her hair. I reached for her, and she squeezed my hand. When Kiril did the same, she flinched from his grasp.

"One Thursday evening, after the other musicians ordered, I placed my order for kids' chicken fingers, the secret order that would alert Ramon it was for me. When the waitress delivered our food, however, she placed kids' chicken fingers in front of me. I asked her if Ramon had sent these out—I was sure it was a joke—and she told me Ramon had been let go, then rushed to a table of hotel guests.

"The other musicians teased me for months after that. They called me 'Kid's Meal' or 'Happy Meal'—I don't remember which—and I deserved it. I never shared with them the special meals from Ramon. It didn't seem right to give them what was cooked only for me. That night, when I received the chicken fingers, I did not go to the garden to wait for Ramon, as some women might have, deluded into thinking it had been some awful mistake. The kid's meal was already humiliating. I would not wait for a ghost. I spent a sleepless night on my cot, in the single room I shared with four other musicians, trying to summon the taste of Ramon's final meal: a seared ahi tuna steak. It was a perfect cut of fish. And he dressed it with a jalapeño and cilantro tapenade that tasted fresher than sunlight. The meal was entirely flavor. Some part of me must have suspected this meal would be my last—Ramon was always fighting with the head chef—and I ate it so slowly, so diligently, that the other musicians returned to our room before I finished. Each bite was smaller than the bite before it, because I wanted to have just completed the meal when Ramon ended his shift, I wanted, when we kissed, for him to taste what he had prepared for me, this meal even he couldn't eat."

No one had ever been as proud of herself as Desi was then. She ignored my glances; she was still at the hotel in Riyadh, locked in that reverie of longing. Eventually, Kiril reached for the fish—each piece now chilly and slick—but Desi slid the plate to the edge of the table, tipping it onto the floor.

The phone calls started at 7:00 a.m. I slept through the first three and would've slept through the fourth, but Desi shouted at me from my bed, in Bulgarian, too exhausted and hungover to switch into English. She had refused to go home with Kiril last night, so I invited her to stay with me. I gave her the bed as a gesture of kindness, she believed, when truthfully I preferred the couch. I'd continued sleeping there, even with the studio to myself.

I thudded off the couch and onto the floor, into the sprays of sunlight pouring through the balcony door. Outside, Vivien was smoking. My phone rang a fifth time. Desi switched to English: "Will you please answer your phone," she said. I lumbered to the glass door, shockingly nude, and shut the blinds before quickly wrapping a blanket over my shoulders. The phone tumbled out from inside the blanket. I missed the call.

It was my mother. As soon as the call ended, the texts began dinging. *Call me!* she texted. My vision was softly glazed like a donut, and I peered at the phone, waiting for the next call to arrive.

I answered on the first ring.

"I've been calling all morning," she said.

"It's still early here," I said.

"How are you possibly sleeping?"

"Everyone has to sleep," I said.

"I hope you weren't drinking. You sound like you were drinking."

"I was trying to take my mind off of things."

"Do you not understand the gravity of what's happened?"

"You didn't have to call me at seven a.m.," I said. Years of tension rushed in like flames through a burning house. Her comments were intrusive the way only a mother's comments can be. I would've hung up if I wasn't sure she would call me right back.

"Five times," she said. "Five times you ignored me."

"I'm assuming you have something to tell me," I said.

"Elizabeth, I need to know I can count on you."

"I have a lot to do today," I said.

"I thought the school gave you off?"

The familiar petulance of my tone—so common to our argument—risked exposing me, so I said what only Elizabeth would in this situation: "I have writing projects to finish."

"This is what I'm talking about," she said. "Your husband is missing and you're trying to write. It doesn't make any *sense* to me. It's—no I won't say it. But I haven't slept since Tuesday. It's sociopathic, that's what it is. Forgive me but that's what it is, just plowing ahead like this."

"There is no right way to grieve."

"I can't eat a single thing. Not a thing. I've been spooning peanut butter into my mouth because I need the calories. Nothing else will stay in me. I haven't even cooked. And as you know—Eli must've told you—cooking is the only thing that eases my mind."

"I'm hanging up," I said.

"He used my credit card," she said.

"Who used it?"

"Why do you think I'm calling you?"

"Of course," I said. I apologized. I sat on the couch.

"He bought drinks at a hotel in Paris."

"Eli isn't in Paris," I said.

"The fraud alert tells me he is," she said.

Behind me, Desi stirred on the bed.

"When did you file the missing person report?"

I hadn't filed one yet.

She shouted: "This is my only child! Do you even love him?"

Her possessiveness was absurd but so authentic, and I felt sorry for her, then sorry for myself: It shouldn't have taken something so drastic for me to see how deeply she cared.

Desi leaned over the couch and spoke into my free ear: "I'm going home."

"You know what—don't answer that," said my mother.

Vivien pounded on the balcony door. I stood, still wrapped in the blanket, and lifted the blinds. Smoking the nubby remains of her cigarette, Vivien pointed at Desi.

My mom screamed, "Do you have any idea how important this is?"

"I'm listening," I told her.

Desi opened the balcony door and exchanged words with Vivien. Desi said to me, "She says to keep your blinds closed when you sleep. She does not want to see you."

"Tell her I'm sorry," I said to Desi. Then I apologized to Vivien through the glass.

"You *should* be sorry for how you've been acting," said my mom.

Desi waved goodbye as she left my apartment.

"I've booked your flight," my mom said. "It's too far for me, at my age. I don't have the stamina to look for him. Plus, I don't know French. I'm not fluent like you."

"You're sure he's in Paris?"

"You're welcome," she said. "Did you hear that I bought you a ticket? A last-minute ticket? Do you have any idea how expensive that is?"

"Thank you," I muttered. She was a stickler for gratitude.

"Your flight leaves this evening at eight." She ended the call.

A burst of knocking rattled the balcony door. When Vivien had my attention, she mimed closing the blinds. I lowered my blanket to the floor and dressed slowly, sliding into sweatpants and a T-shirt as Vivien continued to knock and make a gesture of closing the blinds. Once I was presentable, I stepped to the door, facing Vivien; with a swift tug and a release of the string, I lowered the blinds, separating us for good.

# PART II

The flight landed at six in the morning after a layover in Vienna. I'd told my mother plenty of times that Elizabeth had trouble sleeping, that she spent her nights clawing for scraps between bouts of insomnia. It was not something a mother-in-law would overlook, especially not my mother, who was prone to moments of petty resentment. I suspected that she had booked the overnight flight knowing it would shatter Elizabeth's fragile sleep patterns—payback for not taking my disappearance seriously.

My body hadn't recovered from the night at the fish house. I threw up twice on the plane, and the first thing I did, after passing through customs, was find an unoccupied stall where I could vomit again. There were rules to this body—rules Elizabeth had, over the years, made very clear to me, but hearing her talk about it had been like memorizing the Wikipedia page for a board game, whereas now I was finally playing.

Twelve hours after I landed, I stood looking up into the face of a tall and prickly concierge at the hotel where Elizabeth was staying. Her short, straight hair was the color of figs and stopped—prematurely—at her ears. She did not try to speak to me in French. "Good afternoon, madame," she said, in clipped, impatient English. This offended me. Well, not *me*—I could only obnoxiously pronounce *baguette* and *croissant*—but it would have offended Elizabeth, who studied French in high school and minored in the language at Hinneman. That day, though, Elizabeth was reduced to using my embarrassing English.

The room reserved for me was not yet ready. The guests were staying an additional night. They had a policy, here, where guests could extend their stay up to three nights, no questions asked—of course for a fee—and though the guests rarely took advantage of this opportunity, the people in my room were on their honeymoon and had decided, impulsively, to take another week off work and remain in the city. The concierge appeared sincerely apologetic. The policy she described sounded like a common excuse meant to settle the nerves of new guests when the staff had neglected to prepare their rooms. But I had no reason to argue. Lying—if it was a lie—was part of her job. They were preparing a new room for me as we spoke. It would only be another hour, or two. She offered a voucher for a free drink at the bar to make up for any inconvenience.

At the bar, I ordered the one cocktail Elizabeth normally drank: vodka tonic. And I asked for the "finest vodka you serve" to get the most out of my drink ticket. The bartender was a tired-looking man with thick fingers and a spongy scribble of mustache. I wanted him to make conversation with me, to ask a simple, obvious question—*What brought you to Paris?*—but after serving my drink, he continued prepping the bar for his evening shift.

My mother had left another half-dozen voicemails wanting to know if I'd found Eli yet. Instead of drinking at the bar, I could have asked the concierge if Eli Harding was staying in this hotel, if she could escort me—his wife—to his room. I was, however, scared to disappoint my mother. She wanted something impossible out of this trip. Even if Eli were here, he wasn't her son. It's in my nature to avoid hurting people—which means it is in my nature to do what is most convenient for me, whatever is least likely to result in conflict. Uncovering the truth—whatever the truth may have been—could have only hurt my mother and further complicated matters for me and Elizabeth.

More than disappointing my mother, I feared running into Elizabeth. She had made it quite clear, with her silence, that she did not want to speak to me. I always suspected she would be the one to leave me. At some point, it would occur to her that she had settled, and our love would not seem like a time-less union but a temporary edifice built on a foundation of luck and misfortune—mine and hers, respectively. The Incident had an air of inevitability. This was the universe righting itself. And Elizabeth, it appeared, had listened to what the universe told her. Here was a chance to get out. A chance to never look back. What other conclusion could I draw from her refusal to answer my calls?

"Do you want another?" the bartender asked.

I'd drunk my first one so quickly. "Is it free?" I asked.

The bartender peered around the restaurant. The only other patron was a middle-aged white man in a suit at the end of the bar, typing aggressively on his laptop and sipping something red through a straw. "I will charge it to him," the bartender said.

I laughed and thanked him.

The second drink was stronger than the first—he'd added on to my melted ice—and the alcohol seeped immediately into my cavernous stomach. "How long have you been working here?" I asked.

"Do you really want to know that?" he asked.

"I'm sorry," I said. "I don't." Then I added: "But my husband is gone—" It was the first time I'd spoken that sentence out loud. It didn't sound incorrect.

The bartender did not appear shocked. A hurried and sympathetic compliment wouldn't have helped anything. "You deserve way better," he could have said, intuiting what I didn't feel comfortable admitting, or, "What type of man would leave such a beautiful woman?" These were the very things I would have said—and had said—to the crestfallen people I'd served over the years. Instead, he filled a glass full of water and said, "These things happen quite often."

"I came here to look for him. I know he won't be here but I flew here because I can't not look for him. It wouldn't be right. I should be asking you, now, if you've seen him, that's what someone in my situation should do. It's what someone who loved him would do."

The bartender gave me a cold, quizzical look. This was not an issue of language. He understood what I was saying—and he understood why I was saying it. Not because I wanted to tell *him* but because I needed to tell someone, anyone. I would've confessed to a telephone pole with a face drawn on the side. "Do you want to tell me his name?" he asked.

I didn't. "Eli Harding," I said. "He's about six foot. White. With buzzed brown hair and, most likely, a wispy red beard." Elizabeth hated shaving her legs, and she seemed genuinely concerned for my safety when I razored my face. I doubt she'd shaved since The Incident. "He only ever wears jeans, T-shirts, and sweaters. You may have seen him wearing a yellow crew neck sweater, his favorite. It takes him a long time to warm up to people, so if you saw him you probably saw him alone."

"That could be anyone here."

I thanked him for trying. The man on his laptop flagged down the bartender.

The two men spoke briefly. When he returned, he informed me that the man wished to buy me a drink. We shared a smirk but no laughter. The man in the suit lifted his beer and smiled. *Is this how it happens?* I wondered. I was too tired to find out.

"My room must be ready by now," I said.

The bartender told me he'd be working all night.

Rather than ask the concierge if she could direct me to Eli Harding's room, I instead carried my bag to my room and unpacked. My mother continued to call. I continued ignoring her. But when the caller ID read "Mom," I answered immediately.

"Eli's mother called me," she said. "Is it true?"

"I don't know what she told you," I said.

"You can't go running to Paris for a man who abandoned you."

"What happened to coming to terms with his issues?" I asked.

"What about your issues?"

"I've been wanting to come back to Paris," I said. Surely Elizabeth had mentioned this to her mother. "I've told you that."

"You didn't even tell me you were leaving," she said.

"It all happened so fast," I told her. It hadn't even occurred to me to tell her, and now I was ashamed of myself for forgetting something so obvious. I assured her I wasn't in danger. "Eli's mom bought my ticket and paid for the room. It didn't cost me anything to come here."

"That's not the issue," she said.

"I should've told you," I said.

"That's not why I'm calling." It was well past midnight in Michigan. Elizabeth's parents never stayed up past ten. Commotion filled the space between her words. People were hollering in a language I had only recently begun to register.

"Oh my god," I said. "Why didn't you tell *me*?"

"Your father and I wanted to surprise you," she said.

"Surprise," I said.

"When are you coming back?"

"I need to find Eli," I said. My mother had paid for only four nights in this hotel. I didn't plan on staying any longer than that, but something about the imposition of Elizabeth's parents, their assumption that I would be sitting in the studio, waiting for them, made me protective of my space.

"Your father and I can meet you in Paris."

"I won't be here too long."

"So you know where he is?"

"Eli's mom only paid for four nights."

"Since when do you treat me like an enemy?"

"Since my husband disappeared," I said. Anger tore at the edge of my voice. I had always hated the feeling of someone peering beneath the facade I showed to the world. I liked to present myself on my terms—limited terms. Being seen was an intrusion and especially dangerous now.

"Don't lash out at me, Elizabeth. Your father and I are here because we love you. You know that. Do you think Eli's mother would've flown out to see him if you had gone missing?"

I didn't want to answer that question.

"You're clearly in no mood to hold a civil conversation. You must be sleepless and stressed. Your father and I feel the same way and it's making me harsh. I'm sorry." She paused to leave me room to apologize back.

"Thank you," I said.

"We're going to get a hotel," she said. "I love you."

I told her that I loved her too, and, after we hung up, I couldn't shake what she'd said about my own mother: She was right. She hadn't come looking for me.


THE HOTEL WAS NICER THAN ANYTHING ELIZABETH AND I could have afforded. The room was drenched deeply red, a tone uncomfortably stuck between lavish and seedy, and tangled floral designs were stenciled over the walls. I spread the silver satin curtains, expecting a balcony, but there were no balconies on this floor; the window looked down onto a small stone courtyard. A cherrywood desk was plugged in the corner of the room. On the other side of the room, hulking in front of a tall gilded lamp, were a reading chair and an ottoman, both red with silver arabesques stitched into the cushions. I emptied my backpack onto the king-size bed in the center of the room. I was skilled at making messes of hotel rooms, an absolute expert.

In the bureau, across from the bed, were a robe and a pair of slippers suctioned in plastic. I undressed, then put on the slippers and robe and stepped into the bathroom, a bright marble box with a pristine porcelain bathtub the size of a kiddie pool. It would have given Elizabeth pause. Thousands of businessmen must have showered in here after fucking their mistresses, or had fucked their mistresses in this very tub. This wasn't normally the type of thing that entered my mind—the sex lives of strangers—but Elizabeth and I had taken a weekend trip to Sofia, a month after we arrived in Bulgaria, and that hotel room had had a bathtub, a luxury compared with the showerhead that hung over the toilet in our studio. I suggested Elizabeth take a bath. All month, since we'd arrived, she'd bemoaned not being able to take baths, but she looked at me sideways. "Do you know how many people have fucked in that bathtub?" she asked.

"Let's be happy for them."

"Too many."

I knew she wouldn't have gotten into this tub, if she were here, if she were with me, in her own body. But the stress of the last few months—especially the last week—had taken a toll on her body, the body I was tasked with caring for now. What I brought to the marriage was an impulse to splurge. I brought recklessness. I plugged the drain and started the water. We deserved to relax.

WHEN I GOT OUT OF THE BATHTUB, FIVE NEW VOICEMAILS from my mother were waiting. I promised myself to return her calls once I learned more about Eli from the concierge.

I dressed casually, in jeans and a loose gray sweater and sneakers, planning to explore the city. I would ask the concierge the most basic and unobtrusive questions and accept her professional apologies and go on my way. I owed it to my mother to ask.

But downstairs, a crowd of guests bunched around the front desk. Even if I'd had the patience to wait, I doubted the concierge would have the patience to field my probing and inarticulate questions about a guest. I breezed through the hotel bar to steal a glance at the bartender, but he'd been replaced by a slender blond woman rattling a cocktail shaker over her shoulder. I was disappointed to miss him, and then embarrassed by my disappointment, as if there had been something between us.

Paris was colder than I'd anticipated. The sweater was not warm enough, but I didn't want to venture back for a jacket, though I knew I would need it. The hotel was in the Canal Saint-Martin neighborhood, and everywhere young people were spilled onto the sidewalk smoking and laughing, the type of laughter that only twenty-somethings produce: jagged, careless, detached from their surroundings. It was early evening on a Friday in November. I envied their intimacy, envied those of them eating for crowding together around tables. Elizabeth liked to warm herself against my body on chilly nights. She had thin, delicate fingers that turned blue in the cold, and in the cold she would press herself to me and sneak her hands up my shirt, frigid palms climbing my ribs to my armpits. The shock of her fingers had always disturbed me. But after five minutes outside, my fingers already aching, I understood why she pressed her hands into me, and I wanted desperately to sidle up to a stranger and dip my hands under his shirt.

I missed touch more than anything. Elizabeth and I had spent three years touching each other every day. We were obnoxiously handsy in public. In movie theaters, we would lift the armrest between our seats so that Elizabeth could tangle her legs over mine. On the rare occasions she drank, she loved to make out in public, in dimly lit bar booths or in alleys as busboys hauled out the trash, her hands vining up my spine. We could not pass each other at home without running an arm along the small of the other's back, or over the shoulders, breezing past with silent grazes of longing. The loss of this touch chipped away at something inside me. The instability of this new body, its unfamiliar dimensions, made me long for contact even more, as if this body might collapse without another person holding it up.

I walked through the streets with an unruliness that would not have suited Elizabeth. My arms swung loosely into strangers on the sidewalk. In front of a restaurant called La Fin, I knifed through the line of patrons waiting outside instead of circling into the street to avoid them, inhaling the heady bunch of sweat and cologne and cigarette smoke.

I looked for myself in the faces of passing men: my ridged jawline, the wide drive of my ears. But I was not the right person to look for me. Elizabeth had spent three years looking into my face over coffee and before going to bed. She was more suited to see me than I was. Perhaps she, as me, had unknowingly passed me dozens of times in the hotel, perhaps neither of us was equipped to see themself. I frequently mistook strangers in the street for Elizabeth, sure every petite French woman in a bob was her, though this could not have been more impossible.

After an hour of walking up and down the canal, I settled at one of the few empty restaurants in the neighborhood, a generic, candy-cane-colored spot that advertised crepes and five-euro Stella Artois on the chalkboard outside its front door. I sat at a round metal table beneath an unnecessary umbrella and ordered hot tea and a Nutella crepe. The crepe arrived cold and the Nutella firm, cement beginning to harden. The tea tasted mostly of water, and might have been—there was no bag in sight. The other restaurants overflowed with people eating or waiting to eat, and from the entrance, the waiter watched with his arms tightly crossed. "Does it taste good?" he asked me in English, while holding his gaze on the competing restaurants.

"It doesn't," I said.

He nodded approvingly and slipped back inside.

To anyone passing, I probably appeared on vacation, and a wave of guilt spread through me. I regretted not talking to the concierge. This was not a vacation—this was a search for my missing wife—and I needed to stop treating my time here like a detour from my life.

Sometimes I worried I didn't want to find her, despite how lonely I felt. After three months, I had begun to resent Elizabeth for bringing me to Europe. It was a foolish kind of resentment. It wasn't as if I had some other life waiting for me back in America. I should have been grateful. She was grateful for me. She made this clear when her schedule was especially demanding. On those nights, as she folded over me on the couch to watch a movie, lotioning her shoulders and arms, she would thank me for coming. Specifically: *Thank you for putting your life on hold for me.*

I didn't consider myself capable of providing comfort and assumed that she was lying to me, or to herself, when she made these statements. What other life did she believe I had tabled for her? I had no desire to set out on my own. No original idea had ever occurred to me. Every idea I considered my own was, in fact, an idea I had absorbed from someone else—from a book or a more intelligent friend. I wasn't a person but a protean blob, intellectually and emotionally gelatinous, shaped by whatever surrounded me.

The resentment I had begun to feel in our studio apartment, as I cooked dinners or graded Elizabeth's students' essays—to give her more time to write and to live—was an unfamiliar feeling. It scared me. But I embraced it. I liked the idea that I deserved better than cooking dinners and grading papers, that I was worth more than the life I was living, even if I did, deep down, know this to be false.

That better life, it appeared, was this: an evening alone in a hip Parisian neighborhood at the least trendy restaurant on the block, eating a gluey crepe I couldn't afford. I felt bad about myself and longed to return to the hotel, not to look for Elizabeth but to burrow beneath the covers while watching subtitled French television. I raised my arm to ask for the check, but before the waiter noticed, a hand lowered mine to the table.

Louis, the bartender from the hotel, sat in the chair across from me. "Don't leave," he said. "I've only just got here."

"You told me you were working tonight," I said.

"A friend got me concert tickets."

"Who are you seeing?"

"Some metal band," he said. He named the band and asked if I listened to them.

I told him I didn't.

"It's not my thing but it sounded like a good time—I like an excuse to not work." He lit a cigarette and offered one to me. It was selfish to smoke in Elizabeth's body. But rude to decline Louis's offer.

I took the cigarette in my mouth and leaned forward for him to light me. I was new to using her body this way—as something to be wielded, to be desired—and I liked how it felt. Every time I tried performing hotness in this way as a man—removing my shirt dramatically at a beach, doing sit-ups at a gym, pushing a lawn mower, which I once was told women loved—it had ended in embarrassment. I would trip over my feet as I peeled off my shirt, or unthinkingly run over a branch, causing the mower to rattle and smoke. There was something absurd about a man being hot—at least, something absurd about me trying to be hot. I was overweight as a child, and the idea that my body, once so repulsive to my peers, might evolve into something sexy seemed foolish, unlikely at best. Elizabeth was subtle; being attractive came naturally to her. Louis lit me, grinning.

He laughed. "You don't smoke."

I coughed in response. "Not as often as I would like."

"No Americans smoke," he said. "You all think it's dirty. You're all so sure of your habits—I don't understand."

"We're an exceptional people," I joked.

"You are what?"

"Never mind," I said. I didn't feel like explaining. "Shouldn't you get to your concert?"

"Not if you want to hang out with me," he said.

"You're so rich you can skip it?"

"My friend can find someone else," he said. "I've already gotten what I want from the night: I do not have to work."

"Why come on to me now?" I asked.

"You were sad earlier," he said. "About your husband. Is he still your husband?"

"As far as I know," I said.

"Why are you not with him?"

"Don't make me say it again."

"Hmm," Louis said. We smoked our cigarettes silently, to the nubs. "Well, are we hanging out with each other or not?"

"What do you think?" I asked.

"Then you should pay for your meal."

I liked being told what to do by Louis. Elizabeth often told me what to do, but with her it was different—she directed me through disappointment and exasperation. Louis's demands were exciting, and I felt pleasantly demeaned by his desire. I flagged down the waiter and paid.

"You are looking for something," Louis said when we stood.

"What do *you* think I'm looking for?" I asked, trying to meet his flirtation.

"That is why I asked. A fancy bar? A cheap bar? Or do you want someplace to eat? I know every place in Paris."

"Fancy bar," I said flatly. I was embarrassed to have read his tone wrong. "Wait—trendy. Take me where everyone's going. Take me someplace where we won't get in."

"What's the point?"

"I want you to get us in anyway," I said. "Use your connections."

Louis and I walked for twenty minutes or so until we reached a cocktail bar where, according to him, a friend of his worked. We smoked a few more cigarettes on the walk, and by the third I wasn't making a fool of myself. Throngs of people were cluttered outside wielding drinks and cigarettes. A soccer game blasted on the TV behind the bar, and I squinted to see who was playing but couldn't make out the teams from this distance.

"Wait here," Louis said. He sliced through the crowd and into the restaurant. Minutes later, he returned holding two stubby glasses half-full of a wood-colored liquid. "Boulevardier."

"I can't accept a drink from a stranger," I said. "You might have drugged it." I was teasing him the way I'd seen women tease men in movies, and I took to the performance easier—and more eagerly—than I expected.

"Poison?" he asked. He spoke as if date rape had never reached this country. "No, no, no," he added, with gentle force, twisting his head in emphasis. Strands of hair slipped loose from whatever product was supposed to stay them, then dangled in front of his eyes. He took a generous gulp from one glass, then gulped from the second and combined the two drinks in the first glass. He slid it into my palm and nodded before slipping back for another.

Since boyhood, I latched onto boys I believed were cooler than me, feeling for them a mix of admiration and desire that manifested in a kind of grasping emulation. I was skilled at locating cool boys and ingratiating myself into their lives, adopting their mannerisms, wearing similar clothes, making jokes I knew they would like, revolving around these boys like a small, incapable moon.

Cool boys caught on to me quickly. They tired of my presence once it became clear that I said only what they wanted to hear. They didn't mind being complimented—but they hated when those compliments came from someone they saw as beneath them. During the final week of seventh grade, for instance, after a full school year hovering around a few cool boys in my grade, they sat me down in the cafeteria before the school day began. All the middle schoolers congregated in this room to wait for first period to begin. It was a nothing time of the day. A time for jokes and card games and bagged breakfasts and scrambling through the final few answers of homework—or finding someone to copy. The cool boys had something to tell me. They asked me to sit alone on one side of the table. They lined up on the other side, five cool boys shoulder to shoulder like judges.

That morning, they made it clear they would never hang out with me ever again. They had prepared a list of grievances in a notebook: I invited myself to their houses, ate too many cookies at lunch, laughed too loudly, never made out with girls, was too fat to play paintball, too poor of a shot, too poor to buy an appropriate gun, always choosing the same color paints as everyone else, too polite in front of their parents, too rude in front of their parents, I wore the same American Eagle sweatshirt as Pete on the day Pete wore it, never brushed my teeth—but I did brush my teeth, I said—never brushed my teeth well enough, and, most damning, I drifted into them when we walked together in the hallways, walking at an angle rather than straight as I listened in on their conversation, trying, essentially, to get to the center of the group, to where I didn't belong. The cool boys advised me to take my own life. Somehow, I didn't. But from then on I treated every person I admired or loved with paranoia, waiting for them to turn against me after unrolling a scroll outlining my every act of misconduct.

My feelings for Louis seemed different. I didn't want to emulate him so much as I wanted to be closer to him, to impress him, simply for him to like me and for him to want those same things of me: a desire to be closer, a desire to impress me. Was it as simple as longing for touch? It was, and was more. I could tell he wanted those things of me. He wanted something else from me, too, that I didn't quite understand, or didn't understand how to navigate in this new body, something that Elizabeth surely would have known how to deflect or invite, and I was excited by not knowing how best to act.

Louis returned with another boulevardier. We clinked, and he guided me to a quieter patch of sidewalk, away from the crowd.

"Are you going to tell me why you're here?"

"I told you in the hotel," I said.

"You told me your husband is here. That doesn't explain why you're here."

"It's a complicated marriage," I said.

He absorbed this information. "I'm a handsome man," he finally said. "All American women want a handsome French man."

I laughed uncomfortably. I had never been so brazen in front of a woman I wanted to sleep with. "Is that supposed to impress me?"

"I do not want my time wasted—I skipped the concert, remember? I want this to be a good night for us both." He angled his body away from me, toward the crowd at his back. He could have easily drifted into the mass of people behind us, he could have escaped to the concert—it likely wasn't too late. His presence was a favor to me. He had expectations.

This arrangement made me uneasy; it made me feel vulnerable, and predictable. So I lied to him. "The truth is I abandoned my husband to come here. I asked you about him at the bar because I was nervous he'd follow me here—I wanted to know it was safe. We've only been married four months. But he bores me."

"You left your husband because he bores you?"

"I thought he was smarter and more handsome than he actually is. But we moved to Bulgaria together, in August, right after we married." I answered before he could ask. "We moved for work—my work—and all he does is sit at home and become stupider and fat. Three months and I'm already repulsed by him. I should be moony with love. I should fawn over him, always. But he does nothing to make himself lovable or attractive. I work all day. He reads and watches pornography. He says he doesn't—watch porn—but I know that he does, because he never wants to have sex with me. Me! I'm a good-looking woman." I spoke from some deranged angle of truth. Anyone would've assumed I wasn't good enough for her. I was a waiter when we met, I wasn't in grad school, I had never published my writing. Surely she could do much better than me. She never said this outright, but I feared someday she would un-furl a personal scroll of resentments. Unloading these anxieties on Louis was therapeutic. I wasn't paranoid! Perhaps this was how Elizabeth felt. Perhaps I repulsed her. Perhaps she knew I watched porn, even though I assured her I didn't. Perhaps I was an incompetent lover unaware of my fortune: I was married to a brilliant and beautiful woman.

Beneath the paranoia, though, was the undeniable truth of my opening comment: Elizabeth had left her husband. As ab-surd as it was, I couldn't help believing that she was behind The Incident. Not consciously. But her feelings were powerful—she was ambitious—and if she wished to leave her teaching posi-tion, which she threatened to do every day, I might have been the collateral damage.

"You are very forward," Louis said. He brought his hand to my elbow.

"I'm not," I replied. I had opened a door between us. Now I wanted it shut. "I don't want what you think I want."

"Then what do you want?"

I considered this question for what felt like the first time in my life. I blundered through half answers torn from other people's lives, from Elizabeth's vision of our future, and every response seemed either too false or mundane. Finally, I decided on something—rather, I accepted it, this thing that I wanted, and I leaned close to Louis, my mouth nearly touching his ear to ensure that he would hear me.

Before I could speak, the shooting began.

They met in a state where Elizabeth never expected to live: Arizona. She moved to a city of dust storms and empty skies and roadrunners and heat. She had come there to attend a graduate program for writers, intent on making no friends and completing her book, a novel she had been writing for nearly two years.

The university was notorious for its shirtless, beer-bonging freshmen and a pool the size of a meteor crater, and when Eli arrived, as a freshman, he imagined himself slipping painlessly into a world he already knew. What he found, instead, was a hulking library built in the '50s, dusty and decaying, a refuge from a life, he soon learned, he'd never actually wanted. He was a good student—not like Elizabeth, who envisioned and re-imagined, who earned the respect of her professors—good the way anyone can be a good student: by doing what everyone told him. He completed his homework. He raised his hand. He read the books offhandedly mentioned in classes. He wrote—about his life, his childhood—and he discovered that his life was not everyone's life but a disturbing and curious thing that inspired judgmental awe from professors and classmates. "You have a gift for writing," he was told, by professors who told this to every student who earned As in their classes. But Eli had never been told he was gifted, so he mined this gift through four years of college, scooping out memories like the green meat of an avocado. When the four years ended, adrift, he took a job serving drinks at a big barn of a restaurant at the edge of campus. It wasn't a good job, though it wasn't bad enough to quit, and unwilling to return home to New Jersey, he remained, getting by, writing on the side to nurture his "gift," occasionally checking in with the professors who had praised him, professors who greeted him excitedly, then wistfully, then curiously, before eventually forgetting his name.

Elizabeth settled for this institution, ashamed but too proud to admit it. She deserved better than a state school. But this school offered more money than the other schools that had accepted her, and after four years at Hinneman, surrounded by equally brilliant and capable students, and after three years in the "real world" hopping between appointments and jobs, she longed for the comfort she remembered from youth: being smarter than everyone else in her life.

The night she met Eli, her "cohort"—a term she despised— all went out to celebrate the last Friday night before classes began. She didn't want to go out, but everyone was; she planned to avoid them once the school year commenced, when she could use classwork as an excuse to focus on writing, and she owed it to herself to have some fun before then. The cohort gathered at a sports bar called The Cat's Tongue, after the university's

Bobcat mascot. The temperature had climbed sluggishly into the hundred and teens, and the writers wore tank tops and T-shirts and dresses cut high up the thigh.

They were young and beautiful, full of sex, compassion, laughter, and envy.

Elizabeth wore a breezy, salmon-colored dress cut suggestively to the center of her chest. She didn't have cleavage, but she had collarbone, and, exposed appropriately, collarbone was far more suggestive—it attracted the people she wished to attract, weeded out the ones she did not. At twenty-five, she was the oldest among the writers. The others arrived at the university straight from their undergraduate institutions looking for the continued protections that only college can offer: to stretch their youth taffylike further into their twenties.

The writers settled around a blank red table in the back of the bar, close to a pair of arcade games and a pinball machine. Elizabeth sat beside a twenty-two-year-old poet named Malcolm, who wore a torn green T-shirt and pale cutoff jeans. He spoke with a deliberate tone that suggested unknowable grief. There was something classic and lost about his handsomeness, like a young man who died fighting unhappily for the Confederate Army. His was a face fit for daguerreotype. When he spoke, people listened, because he had earned the right of attention from his appearance alone. No one could imagine him not having something to say.

They'd shared only a few words during their weeklong teaching orientation, and she was excited to talk one-on-one.

He seemed compelling in ways the others were not. The others were open, and nervous; he had something to hide. In friendly settings, she took it upon herself to unravel people's defenses, less a tabby pawing a mouse than a flytrap inviting a gnat.

Years of being the smartest person in rooms made her impatiently curious and cruel on the subject of others' lives. She abhorred small talk and eluded it like a superstitious child leaping over cracks in the street. She skipped past pleasantries to get to The Good Stuff, the fears and shames and joys that separated a person from people. Persons, she liked. Individual persons, persons with complicated and unsettled lives who tried to figure things out. People, however, she could never respect. People loved icebreakers. People mistook graphic designers for artists. People enrolled in burlesque classes and left feeling *so* secure in their bodies. People pet dogs in the street and referred to them as good boys. People discussed the TV shows they were watching. People loved bar trivia and had the funniest name for their team. People admired the narrative power of video games. No, she couldn't stand people. And in social gatherings, like this one, she was skilled at sniffing out people, like a Doberman hunting drugs in the airport.

"When was the last time you cried?" she asked Malcolm.

"Yesterday," he said flatly. "Yesterday morning." Then he turned to the woman on the other side of him to begin a new conversation.

This was, to Elizabeth, the greatest sign of an unconventional mind—the dismissal of her question. He was above her and wouldn't pretend otherwise. Flummoxed, upset, she turned to her right, to the arcade games, where a stranger was playing Big Buck Hunter alone.

His hair was thick and hickory-colored, flopping on top of his head—it was the longest it had ever been and would ever be. The following day, he would shave it himself after weeks of pressure from his boss to get a haircut. He'd come here straight after an early shift and was still wearing his work jeans, though he'd traded his uniform polo for a wrinkled white T-shirt. Elizabeth noticed his height. She didn't like that this was important to her.

"Is this rifle taken?" Elizabeth asked, lifting the orange gun from its holster.

"I reserved it for you," he said. Then Eli told her his name.

"You fit so nicely in mine," she said. "Elizabeth." She aimed the orange rifle at the screen, where deer pranced Bambi-ishly through a forest. "How does this work?" she asked.

"Are you one of those women?" he said.

"What type of woman?"

"The type who pretends they know less than they do."

She blushed, but recovered. "I know I'm going to wreck you," she said. "If that's what you're asking. But I thought I'd give you a chance to sabotage me."

"Aim for the sun," he said. "And the sky and the trees. Whatever you do, don't try shooting the bucks."

She thanked him.

"How many quarters do you have?" He was down to his final one. They needed a dollar's worth to play. She bent over her chair and hunted through the change pouch in her purse. Inside were three quarters, nothing else, and though, if pressed, she would never have admitted to believing in fate, she wasn't opposed to the concept in convenient, night-altering doses. She showed the quarters to Eli. They played. He destroyed her.

"So this is your move, huh?" she said. "You sucker women into feeding you quarters and get off on embarrassing them?"

"Most women don't see through me so quickly."

Elizabeth peered back at the table of writers, all of whom were discussing things she couldn't pretend to care about. They gossiped about classes, about the programs they'd declined, the ones who declined them. "Buy me a drink?"

She waited for him in a booth. He returned with a vodka tonic inside a glass stein. He was drinking a beer. "You're gonna get me drunk," she said, suddenly nervous.

"My buddy's the bartender," he said. "He's always giving me massive drinks—it's a sign of affection." He jumped up and returned with two waters. "This better?"

It was. She took a sip of her drink through its pitiful cocktail straw. Then she asked Eli the same question she'd put to Malcolm.

"I'm crying right now," Eli said. "I can't believe you're not comforting me."

She smirked. It was funny, but not in a humorous way. His self-centeredness intrigued her—she didn't like this part of herself, the part that was intrigued by self-centered people. In the past, a friend concluded that she would always surround herself with interesting people rather than nice people, and this remark cut her for reasons she did not wish to explore. This friend was a boyfriend and shortly thereafter an ex. He was correct, but he was also nice, and, according to his own theory, that meant he had to go.

"I like seeing men cry," she said.

"Women hate seeing men cry," he said. "There's nothing more terrifying for them."

Surely other things scared her more than men crying. Men killing, for instance. Men raping. Men outside your house uninvited. Though she pondered the statement and landed, unexpectedly, on a memory of a male friend, in high school, crying after his grandfather died, and how wretched she felt trying to comfort him, how the sight of his pain scraped under her skin like a fingernail, until she made an excuse about basketball practice—something obviously false—to escape from him. She had never seen her father cry, or her brother, and she realized, then, that she wanted nothing more than to keep it that way.

"When did you last cry?" he finally asked.

"That's none of your business."

"That's why I asked."

She surprised herself by answering honestly. A month earlier, in Athens, she had cried in a hostel bathroom after fucking a lover. They became close friends in college and dated periodically—unenthusiastically, really—but after fucking in a dusty hostel room, on the bottom bunk of a bunk bed, she felt a suffocating tenderness from him. She only agreed to come on this trip after clarifying that they did not love each other—not in that way—that they were friends who cared deeply for each other and were mature enough to understand sex didn't mean love. She felt betrayed by his affection. She admired this man—a brilliant friend, a man who would go on to engineer an app that made him millions of dollars—and could never pretend that she loved him. She respected him too much to lie. In the bathroom, still warm from sex, her face flush, she cried because they had four days left on the trip, and she knew, then, that despite the burden and cost, she would fly home the next morning, that she would lie to protect his feelings—his small, innocent feelings—her vacation over, their friendship cracking like a layer of ice over a lake.

She did not say all of this. She said, "A month ago, in Athens, saying goodbye to a friend from college."

"There's more to that story," said Eli.

She liked that he could see a part of her she did not want to disclose.

They made out in the parking lot. He came home with her. She wasn't a one-night-stand kind of woman, so, to prevent herself from becoming one, she asked for his number in the morning. A week later he took her out for falafel at a Middle Eastern restaurant tucked behind a bodega. They had sex that night and the following morning, then later that afternoon, and by the following week her roommate was asking, "So are you and that waiter 'a thing'?" Elizabeth shrugged the question away, briefly embarrassed to hear Eli reduced to "that waiter." Wasn't she better than that?

Eli did not hide his feelings. Like most men who feel strongly for women, he pursued her in bold and claustrophobic ways.

He bought her books he thought she would like, he burned her CDs, he texted to ask what she was doing throughout the day, he invited himself over to her apartment, proceeded to cook her a confusingly bland meal of chopped spinach over pita, a meal Elizabeth had never encountered and would never encounter again. He shared stories of childhood trauma without prompting. As Elizabeth listened to him, her feelings sloshed inside her like so much curdling milk, and when he finally stopped, she buried the details at the bottom of her brain so as not to tarnish the picture of him she wished to create.

They saw each other sparingly. Elizabeth had a novel to write, and she couldn't visit his restaurant or hang out after his shifts. Nonetheless, she felt special around him—reluctantly special—and kept a lock on her feelings, protecting them, until the evening her roommate confessed to having a crush on Eli—based only, it appeared, on the night he'd cooked his baffling spinach pita. She had overheard his confessions from her bedroom. "He's so honest," she said.

Elizabeth was foremost a feminist, and she did not like the idea of competing with another woman over a man, but she was also a feminist, and nothing, she believed, should stand in the way of meeting her sexual needs.

Elizabeth had never not won. But her prize—she had to accept—was Eli, a man who, after weeks of making out and fucking in her bed (his was too small, his apartment too far out of town) asked her what she thought about dating exclusively. Her true feelings? She felt okay about that. Not bad and not great. A mere middle of longing.

Only two months into The Program, the other writers were already coupling up. Their relationships reminded Elizabeth of pieces fitting from separate puzzles, the parts locking together as the images clashed. She did not want to participate in that. Rather than dating someone because she saw him every day in class, allowing repetition to sand away at her standards, she would, instead, subvert the trends of her peers.

She admired Eli's feral relation to writing, so different from the anxious, zip-hoodie drive of the men in her program, writing in search of A-pluses and professors' pats on the head. She longed for these things herself and had no intention of changing. How wonderful it was to see Eli, then, collecting scraps of free time to build a writing career like a crow making a nest out of napkins and straws. Was he a good writer? Why even ask such a question? He loved it, and love, she was learning, was rare.

So she silenced the voice in her head wishing that Eli were better, wishing he had stronger social graces and had attended a higher-ranked school. They bonded over sentences. She had never been around another person who felt the kind of radioactive desire for language she had felt her whole life. In bed, they tangled together like wires behind a TV, reading aloud from books they admired. She read to him from an uncanny work of prose by a French surrealist that was as refractive and bright as a geode while remaining as light as a lie. He read to her from a novel about a boy who worked at a butler academy. He was drawn to the narrator's aspiration to "be nothing." He considered this profound. She considered it troubling. He valued moments of arbitrary existence; he expected to be forgotten; he invited mediocrity into his life like a vacationing cousin. Truthfully, he feared being forgotten but understood everyone would, eventually. He confronted this fear by pretending he longed to be small.

Elizabeth knew only ambition. Eli lived on the bridge between ambition and leisure. His ambition was leisurely, his leisure ambitious. Perhaps it was a good thing? He wasn't constantly going. Perhaps he could balance her out.

After a year of dating, Eli took the roommate's place in the apartment. Neither he nor Elizabeth had ever lived with a partner—a word that both of them hated, a word glazed with the propriety of academe and the ruthlessness of corporate sharks—and rather than let the pressure unsettle them, they treated this next step in their lives, their cohabitation, as a fun challenge to their prior conceptions of self.

The challenge challenged them more than they liked. But in many ways, it protected them from their most harmful instincts. Elizabeth learned to stop working into the wee hours. Previously, she would drill over the same two sentences late into the evening, as ten became eleven became midnight then one, and she'd have to scrape herself away from the screen. In these private sprees of obsessions, she could go without meals and exercise as her eyes hardened to stones. Another person in the house who insisted on sharing things with her—his meals, his body—forced her outside her head at respectable times, though she suspected she loved the drain of obsession more than she loved the person sharing her bed.

Eli, for his part, had a history of throwing up after meals—he'd thrown up often during their first year together, when he came home after a date to the small room and bathroom he rented—though, in Elizabeth's apartment, with Elizabeth there in the mornings and there in the afternoons and there in the evenings, always at her desk writing, Eli had no time to throw up his meals. He couldn't lie in the ways he'd become accustomed to lying. Elizabeth knew about the eating disorders, and she loved him, and thus she worried about him, and had he thrown up in the bathroom they shared she would have intervened. The only thing worse for Eli than absorbing the calories he consumed was explaining to someone who loved him why he threw up.

He believed that he didn't like to be cared for in this manner. He believed himself above the love of others even as he desired their unadulterated attention. Moving in with Elizabeth cut down on the time available to harm himself. This was how relationships worked for men: When they grew closer to someone who did not want them to die, they had to confront the many ways they were killing themselves. It pained Eli to lose these moments of harm. He loved harming himself more than he loved himself, more than he loved Elizabeth, a truth too dangerous to approach, as if it were a snarling dog about to escape from its collar.

It was this impulse to harm himself that led Eli into the arms of a co-worker one evening after his shift. They didn't fuck. But they came close. Elizabeth found out from a friend of Eli's who had—inexplicably, she thought at the time—invited her out to coffee. Elizabeth thanked the friend, too shocked to show any emotion, and returned to the apartment where she systematically boxed up Eli's possessions. She was not the type of woman to toss things on the lawn. He found her in the living room, on the couch behind the castle of boxes, and proceeded immediately to apologize. He wept. He begged. And she pitied him. She had always pitied him, had always liked it a little too much, having this power over a man. Worse, she liked having him around. She made demands. He agreed to nearly all of them—except quitting his job; there were too few restaurants in town that paid a livable wage—and reenrolled in therapy to figure out his shit, in her words. "I don't normally do second chances," she said. He thanked her, from his place beside her on the couch. "Don't you dare embarrass me like this ever again."

She did not help him unpack.

# PART III

In the rush of getting away from the attacks—we were only three blocks away—I tripped over a toppled chair and scraped open my palms. Louis bled from a long scratch on his forearm, though he had no memory of cutting himself.

We ran another ten blocks before we felt safe enough to stop outside a nondescript bar with a name I cannot remember. Word of the attacks had already arrived via phones and the sight of people sprinting away from the violence. A couple sitting at a table on the sidewalk asked us what had happened. It was a man and a woman, the man much older than she was, and he patiently sipped his drink as he awaited an answer. His composure would later disturb me. Why weren't they running to their apartments? What made them so confident in their safety?

Louis answered the man in French. I told the couple that I heard shooting and that it sounded so real, even more real than I expected shooting to sound.

Louis and I were now an attraction, and everyone at the bar was coming outside to crowd around us, desperate for details. Louis drifted down the sidewalk, swallowed by familiar Parisians. The English speakers tightened around me—Brits, Germans, an American stray. I was pleased to separate from Louis. Trauma either zips people together or heaves them apart, and we were better suited for the latter.

"It sounded like guns do in movies," I said. "But that can't be right—movies aren't supposed to be accurate."

One British man looked at me sternly. "It wasn't a movie."

Even in shock, I wanted to shout at him. Did he think I was stupid? Of course I knew it wasn't a movie. "I'd never heard guns fired in real life," I said, through my teeth.

I was shaking, or so I discovered, when a woman draped her arm over my shoulder. "Let's get you inside," she said.

Inside was long and skinny like a train car. Small round tables were pushed against the wall across from the bar. I followed the woman to a horseshoe booth at the back, lit seedily beneath a breath of red lighting. Her friends were packed around the table. I felt as if I had only just landed on earth from some other planet. My palms continued bleeding. I kept wiping them dry on my sweater, and my injuries appeared more gruesome than they were as my palm prints dried maroonly over my breasts.

I was given a seat at the head of the table, where I proceeded to ramble and shiver. Everyone in the bar offered me coats, and I overheated beneath the layers, though I refused to take any off. I liked being a coatrack for their compassion.

The Brits in the bar, anxious to hear what happened to me, were the true experts among us. What I had was experience, and fear, but experience and fear were not knowledge, as badly as we all wanted them to be. All I knew was how it felt to scramble away from the shooting, the sound of shattering glass and shattering screams. The Brits knew that mine hadn't been the only attack. The shootings were coordinated, they said. The attackers were part of a global terrorist network—without evidence, the Brits claimed that these people had entered the country using refugee status.

Being at the center of something enormous often means you're the last person to make sense of what happened. Understanding is for outsiders. The Brits told me how many were dead and where the dead had been killed. They told me a police response was currently underway and that the suspects remained at large in the city. They told me we shouldn't be out right now, not according to the police, and believed that being out might be the safest place, that it was highly unlikely other bars would fall prey to the same attackers tonight.

I told them that I had been scared. I told them that I had run.

"That must have been so terrifying," they said, over and over again.

"I'm so glad you made it," they said.

"So many didn't," they said.

They read news reports aloud from their phones. Incrementally, I came to understand the gravity of what had happened that night, how lucky I was to be alive, how intensely I wanted to be away from them and with Elizabeth. I needed to know she was safe. If she truly was in Paris, she might have been wounded. Or killed. "I need to leave," I said and rushed out of the bar, draped in layers of coats.

THE HOTEL HAD NO RECORD OF ELI HARDING. OR ELIJAH Harding. Or Elijah David Harding or any of the other variations I proposed to the increasingly impatient concierge. "You might try checking tomorrow," she said, passing my urgency onto a colleague.

What were you doing out?" Johanna asked on the phone the following morning.

"I can't stay in my room twenty-four-seven," I told her.

"You told us you were only there looking for Eli. He's clearly not in the hotel. It's time to come back."

"I owe it to his mother to keep checking—especially after last night."

"Then we're flying to see you. You shouldn't be alone for this."

"It's better for everyone if I'm alone," I said. I couldn't continue avoiding her parents. At some point, I would have to confront them in person, and my performance over the phone would unravel. This wasn't feasible. But I hoped to have my life—and Elizabeth's life—sorted out by the time I met up with Johanna and Henry.

"I'm booking you a flight back to Bulgaria. You need to come home."

"Bulgaria isn't home," I said, petty in the way only a child can be.

"It's more home than a hotel room in Paris," she said.

After three years of dating Elizabeth, I knew to trust her mother's stubbornness. It had shaped Elizabeth into the person I admired and loved. I could not compete with that kind of drive, but I could deflect—in ways Elizabeth never could.

"It's probably not safe to travel right now," I said. "I heard most outgoing flights have been grounded."

"Where did you see that?" she asked.

"Somewhere," I said. "I don't know. On the news."

"They've probably caught the attackers," she said. "There's no reason to keep people trapped in the country. They're turning you into prisoners."

"I'll look up flights," I said. I was in my hotel bed weighed down by blankets. Last night, draped in coats, I'd entered my room burdened by warmth. I set the air conditioning to its coldest setting and stripped naked to sleep, tossed the comforter to the floor. Throughout the night, the cold air startled me awake; rather than change the temperature I dragged the blankets back into bed and tightened them around me. When the blankets were not enough, I hauled the coats into bed, one then two then three then four until all five were gummed over my body.

"What are you seeing?" Elizabeth's mother asked.

I put her on speaker and made a *hmm* sound like I was searching for flights on my phone. I scrolled past headlines outlining what I had survived.

"I'm not seeing anything," I said.

"Let me look," she said. She must have already been looking, because she immediately added, "I'm seeing one here on Monday. Can you wait that long?"

"I have the room until Tuesday."

"That's not what I asked," she said. "We can rent a car and drive to you."

"Please don't do that," I said. I found an image of a café that Louis and I had passed before stopping at the cocktail bar. I couldn't remember whether he'd suggested that café, or if I'd marked it in my head as a possible option. Both scenarios seemed too convenient. Perhaps my life hadn't been as threatened as every news story made it seem.

"I'm booking this flight for you now," she said.

In the photo, the front window is shattered; every chair inside is toppled.

"I can't wait to see you, sweetie," she said.

"Have you always called me sweetie?" I'd never heard her use the term around Elizabeth.

"Not since you were a baby," she said, a little embarrassed. She apologized and I told her I liked it. After we ended the call, I was alone, again, with my blankets and breeze and images of yesterday's carnage.

I stayed in my hotel room for two days sucking down every story I could about the attack. Fear is an addiction, and it had never been so available to me. I kept the TV on at all hours watching what appeared to be the French version of CNN. Little the newscasters said registered with me. Occasionally, some word shared by English and French—a street name or a landmark or an obvious cognate—would flash like a floodlight flickering on, but I hated those moments, for they broke the spell of paranoia cast by the repetitive carnage, the same twenty seconds of footage on a continuous loop, the words muttered emotionally in a language I could not understand.

I fielded what felt like hundreds of calls from my mothers—Johanna and mine—over the weekend. With the TV muted, I would assure my mom that I was looking for Eli and assure Johanna that I was looking up flights, saying the same thing so often I could have played a recording for them, and once the calls ended I would fall back into the trance of the TV, like a fish being tossed back into water.

On Monday, the reports shifted to Paris reopening—or so I

gathered—and whatever rope that had tied me to the TV suddenly snapped. I felt small and guilty for lying to my mother, so I left my room, intent on being more persistent with the concierge and anyone else in the hotel who may have seen Eli.

LOUIS WASN'T WORKING AT THE BAR WHEN I VENTURED downstairs. I was relieved. What could we have talked about after what we had been through? I was happy to simply disappear from his life.

The bar was overrun with hotel guests fixated on the TVs flashing behind the bartender. They gestured; they wept. They absorbed each other's stories. No one could believe what they'd lived through, and they longed to disperse their fear—and their gratitude, a troubled, guilt-ridden gratitude—onto others until only comfort remained. But there was something temporary and false about their terror. Most people here were guests in this city—they were tourists, and theirs was outsiders' fear, exaggerated and selfish, the kind unique to the safe. Yet they were eager to be part of something enormous. I was, as well. I would've gladly spoken to any one of them about how fortunate I was that it hadn't been me—how close I had been to my end—and how heartbroken I was for those who had not been as lucky. Was it wrong to attach ourselves to a tragedy that wasn't ours? Yes, it was. But in that moment, it seemed we had no other choice.

I felt underdressed in jeans and a sweatshirt. My sneakers were still at the foot of the bed where I'd kicked them off before falling asleep on Friday. Assuming I'd face the same empty bar from my first day at the hotel, I had plodded downstairs in my complimentary slippers. The other guests were in suits or presentable dresses, makeup applied, too put together for the collective anxiety this setting demanded. This was how the wealthy moved through the world. They never went out without suspecting they would be seen. I could have returned to my room for real shoes and a blouse without stains on the collar or even a dress. But that seemed like a concession to the world they'd built in the lobby and bar. I didn't want to give in to that world, so I squeezed through the crowd in search of an open stool.

Only one stool was remaining, and it remained open because the man sitting beside it had spread a large map of Paris over the counter. I asked him if the stool was taken.

"There's nobody sitting there, is there?" he asked. It was the businessman from my first day at the bar. His English was maddeningly perfect, the English of a German, I guessed. His hair was short and blond, and he wore a suit as black as tires. He rapped his muscular fingers over the map and drank beer from a highball glass.

I contorted myself onto the stool. "Excuse me," I said, gently nudging the map with my elbows, to let him know this was my space.

"Pardon," he said, and moved nothing. He took a sip and set down his beer over the Seine, where a dark wet ring wrinkled the paper. It was a tourist map from the front desk. The hotel's insignia appeared on the lower left corner, the corner pointing directly at me. Scattered across the map were large yellow stars marking major attractions and restaurants.

Against my will, I wanted this man to talk to me and was hurt that he hadn't. I wanted the same thing that everyone in this bar wanted: to dilute my trauma with inane conversation. "Is that Paris?" I asked, though it was obviously Paris.

"Can't you see I'm working," he said. With a red felt pen, he drew circles on the map and connected them with dotted lines.

"Are those the sites of the shooting?" I asked.

"My work is very important," he said. "Both to me and to you. To everyone here. It is classified top-level work."

"You're working at a bar," I told him. "It can't be that secret."

"It would be difficult for me to explain," he said.

"I have time."

"Not as much time as you think."

"You're threatening me?"

"My room has been bugged," he said.

This man was a kook. Kooks were my favorite kind of people.

"To answer your question," he said, "that's why I'm here, at the bar. The noise will prevent the microphones from recording my work. Crowds are a perfect disguise."

"But what are you doing?" I needed to know, even if his answer didn't make sense.

"You have to promise not to tell anyone," he said.

"Who would I possibly tell?"

"If they catch you, I mean. If they ask you about me. Do you promise?"

I promised.

"You might be tortured," he added. "For what I'm about to tell you. I should have told you that, before you promised. Do you still promise?"

I promised even harder this time. My impulse to unload intimate details about myself to strangers attracted strangers looking to unload intimate details on me. I was a willing recipient for unhinged monologues. Elizabeth found this part of me tiresome. She insisted it was easy for me to listen to these people—these men, always these men—because they did not want to sleep with me. They didn't assume my listening was a sign that I wanted to fuck. And as the man started to speak, I thought of Elizabeth, wondering whether I should be more cautious, if I ought to have sat here quietly drinking instead of engaging.

"I work in patterns," he told me. "I look for convergences and coincidences—which are never truly coincidences. We should abolish the word from all languages. Did you know that? That coincidences are never truly coincidences?"

"I've heard things," I lied.

"Heard things," he scoffed. "Well, hear this." He tapped his red pen at the center of one of the circles. It was the site of the shooting, close to the bar where Louis and I had been drinking. "And now look here." He tapped the center of a second circle, at one of the other sites of the violence. He drew a hard line between the two circles over the dotted line he'd already drawn. He offered no explanation whatsoever. "Do you see?"

"What am I supposed to be seeing?"

"Pay attention," he said. He drew a line from the midpoint of the line he'd just drawn to the site of the most intense attack of the evening: the venue where the metal band played. It was the show Louis was supposed to have attended, and I shuddered thinking of what he might be going through now, the likely death of his friends, the guilty relief he must be feeling.

The man drew a line from the stadium to the Eiffel Tower, then a line to the Louvre, a line to Notre Dame, concluding with a line to the Arc de Triomphe. "Now do you see?"

"Yes," I lied, because I didn't want him to tell me to pay attention again.

"Pay attention," he said. "You don't see anything because there's nothing to see. I've been working in patterns for half of my life and I've never seen anything like this. Nothing. No pattern. No coordinated sense of structure. No focus on major tourist locations. It's as if they attacked on a whim."

"They attacked the concert," I said. "And that stadium. Clearly that took some planning."

"What I'm trying to tell you is that it isn't like patterns not to have patterns. There is no pattern. And if there is no pattern, then the next attack could be anywhere."

"Even here," I said.

He grinned. "Exactly."

I should have congratulated this man on his findings and wished him a good day. But of all the people in this city he seemed the most likely to believe The Incident had occurred. Perhaps he could explain what had happened to us. "I have something to tell you," I said.

"I'm very busy," he said.

"It's about patterns," I said.

He looked at his watch. "We should get out of here. The guy at nine o'clock is leaning a little too close for my liking. I'm going to pay using cash and quietly leave. Do not say goodbye. Do not look at me as I depart. Meet me outside in five minutes. If I'm not there, then we have been compromised. Meet me in my room at eight forty-seven p.m."

"Is that what this was about?"

"I can't believe you would accuse me of something so crass," he said. "I haven't had sex in forty-three years."

I apologized.

He slid his room card across the map and proceeded to fold the city into a wadded wet square. It fit thickly in his suit jacket pocket.

"Isn't your room bugged?"

"Eight forty-seven exactly," he said. "Not a second later." He placed a twenty-euro bill on the counter. "À bientôt!" He waved to the bartender as he left.


FIVE MINUTES LATER, I SLID THE MAN'S KEYCARD INTO MY jeans pocket and exited the bar, without having ordered anything. Two armed soldiers stood watch at the entrance to the hotel. Across the street, two more hovered in front of a rival hotel. They wore complete tactical gear, carrying guns the size of greyhounds; their chins stuck out from their bulky helmets like feet kicked through floorboards.

The man from the bar stood in a crowd of smokers outside the hotel with an unlit cigarette sprouting from his lips. "What took you so long?" he asked.

"I had to close my tab," I said.

"You weren't drinking."

"I got something after you left."

"You know we're going to be walking for a while," he said. He nodded at my feet.

I was still wearing slippers. "These are very comfortable."

"You better hope so."

"Can I have one of those?" I gestured toward the cigarette.

"Smoking will kill you," he said. He jabbed his unlit cigarette into the tall plastic ashtray. "Eight forty-seven."

"I thought we were going for a walk."

"You'll slow me down," he said.

"You haven't even told me your room number."

"Pay attention," he said. He stepped into the street and was nearly flattened by a cab. The cab stopped, and he hammered his palm on the trunk to get the driver's attention. The driver stepped out of the car, and the man from the bar gave an apologetic bow. The two men hugged, business-like, then went on with their lives.

I plucked the stubbed cigarette from the ashtray and pulled it taut between three fingers. It worked as well as anyone might expect. A spectral French woman with short black hair joined me. I mimed lighting my crumpled cigarette.

"You know we all speak English," she said. Her first three attempts to light me failed. She lit a fresh cigarette from her pack and passed it to me. I released a storm of coughs after the initial inhale.

"First time?" she asked.

"Fourth," I answered.

The French woman nodded frankly then walked to the other side of the entrance, where a crowd of smokers were smoking in French. I continued smoking and coughing, alone in my slippers, wondering what to do with my life.

Then Eli exited the hotel. He walked toward me, but I spun away as he passed.

He wore a slimming gray suit that looked like it cost a few thousand dollars and walked with a graceful confidence that I had never shown in my life. I was awash in relief—Elizabeth was alive!—which soon dried into confusion, and anger. If she was alive, she should have been searching for me. She should have answered my calls!

I waited until Eli was half a block away before following him. The map man was right—my slippers slowed me down. Worse, they rendered me obvious. Everyone I passed on the street glanced at my slippers with a look of pity. Perhaps they thought I was mentally ill, or lost, or escaped. Thankfully, no one offered to help.

Eli moved with pace and purpose that made him difficult to trail. I always walked faster than Elizabeth, a habit she resented. My pace implied callous self-interest. I didn't care enough about her to walk at an appropriate speed. It was a damning but possibly accurate portrait. I'd treated everyone in my life the same way, charging ahead impatiently, rushing off to wherever I needed to be without considering the needs of others, be they a parent or partner or friend. This led to countless fights in past relationships, though it never truly felt like a problem until this afternoon, as I struggled to keep up with myself, in a body that wasn't my own.

The slippers started showing their quality after ten minutes. They provided absolutely no warmth against the November chill and angled out crookedly every few steps, causing my heels to tap on the sidewalk. This was an expensive part of the city, a part of the city worth protecting, and at every street corner and outside every hotel and every three or four restaurants were armed soldiers prepared for the worst to happen again. They bunched at street corners like malevolent grapes. Lethal and bored, they toed the ground and cracked jokes, craning their heads with sluggish vigilance.

Eli slipped into a coffee shop too small for me to enter unnoticed. It was a nondescript café with a single plate window and walls as blank as wax. At a table in front of the window, two beautiful women smoked beautifully, speaking their beautiful language. I pressed my face to the window and cupped my hands over my eyes to peer inside, trying to see what Eli was ordering.

Normally, I drank black coffee to prevent taking on calories, though Elizabeth preferred lattes. If The Incident had truly occurred, then he would order a latte. Soon, I would have proof. He reached the front of the line. I flattened my nose against the glass. The barista nodded and scurried off to prepare his drink.

"Pardon," said a woman seated at the table beside me. My hip was grazing the table where she sat with her friend. She continued speaking in French, her voice sharp with frustration and dignity, like a chalice brimming with thumbtacks.

I apologized in beleaguered French and the woman continued berating me. She shooed me away. "Une seconde," I said, unsure whether it meant "one second" in French. I held up one worthless finger.

Her friend shooed me as well. But I didn't budge. I peered back inside just as Eli paid the cashier. I stepped a few feet away in the other direction, avoiding Eli as he stepped outside, and in my haste a slipper slipped off. The French woman pointed, demanding that I retrieve the slipper. I ignored her until Eli was far enough away not to hear us, then picked up the slipper, thanking the women as if we were friends, or as if they'd just dragged me out of a burning car, and they looked at me like they were willing a dog bite into my future.

Eli continued at his maddening pace, walking with his head down, narrowly avoiding passersby, twisting his body away as his shoulder brushed theirs. Elizabeth appeared at ease in my body in ways that I'd never been. She proceeded confidently, and I envied her, not only because I struggled to make sense of her body but because it seemed unfair that she might be a better version of me than I'd ever been.

Eventually, the strawlike alleys and streets opened on a grand stone plaza crowded with children and parents pushing strollers. The ground descended at a slight angle, and people were treating the decline like one massive chair, lounging and sharing breakfasts or silently reading alone. On the far side of the plaza was a hulking glass building layered like a napoleon pastry; it appeared under construction, masked in scaffolding. A long glass tube dragged over the front like a segmented seatbelt, flattening at every one of its six floors. Inside the tube, an escalator ferried people upstairs. Eli avoided the children and parents and darted to the closest trash can to deposit his coffee cup. I sunk seeing the cup fall in the trash. There would be no clues to uncover, no shortcuts to understanding—at least, not in what he was drinking. He opened the paper bag and lowered his hand inside. I was an obvious figure, not even a hundred feet from Eli and staring at him, unable to look away. The slightest turn of his head would have exposed me. No person had ever been more visible. He fished his hand around the bag like his keys were lost at the bottom. If he were me—if we hadn't changed bodies—then inside would be a scone or a stub of biscotti. If he were Elizabeth, there'd be a granola bar, maybe a pain au chocolat or an orb of underripe fruit. He freed tufts of napkins from the bag and jammed them into his back pocket. Afterward, he appeared to lose interest in the bag, turning, in-stead, toward the glass building, or the sky above it, where a flock of birds had risen off the roof. Had he really carried a bag full of napkins all this way? I wanted to scream, *Empty the bag!*

He finally pulled out a bottle of water and tossed the crum-pled bag in the trash. It was not a small bottle of water. One liter, at least. Undeterred, he wrapped his lips around the rim and drank, his neck bulging as the water descended his throat, cheeks tightening, nostrils flaring, the water glugging lower and lower as he tipped the bottle higher and higher, his head tilting back as if he were having his hair washed, Adam's apple galloping forward, until the bottle was empty. He dragged his arm over his mouth. The bottle went in the trash.

He entered the building through the doors at the center. I made a wide loop in following him. This route led me right into a cloud of children giggling and jumping beneath a solar system of soap bubbles. A man in blue overalls dipped a giant wand in a kiddie pool of solution and dragged the wand overhead, the bubbles emerging like aliens from a portal. As a child, I had been mesmerized by bubbles. My mother married two more times after my father, each marriage—and divorce—coming before my eleventh birthday, and at every reception she made sure bottles of bubbles were included with the favors. Whenever the guests stood up to dance or get drinks, I would scurry from table to table, stealing the bubbles before escaping outside to blow them alone. This same sense of whimsy overtook me when I entered the crowd of children leaping at bubbles. I was much taller than the children and popped three bubbles easily, setting off a wave of hollering from children and parents alike. The man in the overalls pointed at me in disbelief. I tucked my head under my arm, worried Eli would see me. But he was inside, I reminded myself, and I was free to be my negligent, discernible self—as soon as I thought this, however, Eli emerged from the building doors and walked to the mouth of the escalator tube.

A line of college students stretched out from the end like a snake halfway out of its skin. Bunchy canvas backpacks slouched on their shoulders. They cradled books under their arms. Eli spoke to a woman at the end of the line, then cut ahead of the students in front of him. No one stopped him or cared.

I took my rightful place at the end of the line, envying Eli for cutting. A blocky boy with dark saddles under his eyes turned to face me.

"Bibliothèque?" he asked.

I shook my head. It was one of the few words I believed I knew: bookstore.

"Pompidou?"

This seemed the more likely destination. I nodded.

The boy spoke a full sentence in French, and I promptly registered nothing. He sighed. My need exhausted everyone in this country. "The library does not open until noon," he said. "Go before of us."

I thanked him, nearly bowed. "What floor is the gallery?" I asked.

He stuffed headphones into his ears.

Inside the tube, the escalator was stalled in place. The students squeezed against the railing with their necks curled down into books. I slipped past them, clenching my toes to hold my slippers in place. Not one student remarked on my presence. They were skilled at reducing their surroundings to background noise. I doubt they knew I existed.

Passing them felt like passing a line of souls preparing for purgatory. Elizabeth had a similar life at Hinneman. Like them, she sacrificed her Friday and Saturday nights to the gods of grade point averages. I never did anything like this in college. I spent my weekend mornings dozing through hungover lulls, leaving bed briefly to piss, whereas Elizabeth woke up promptly at eight on weekends to meet the library doors right as they opened. Seeing these students, I pitied the young woman Elizabeth had been. How willing she was to abandon hours of her life, hours that accreted into days into weeks that bundled into entire years she would never get back. Those sacrifices brought her to Europe. She had, after all, received the illustrious fellowship to Bulgaria, teaching English to students who had little desire to learn it, indoctrinating them in American culture to further the aims of the government. She published stories in journals. She fielded emails from agents. She held a degree from an elite liberal arts college, and someday that degree would open doors that mine never could. But was it worth it? It wasn't for me to know.

On the third level, the line of students curved toward the locked doors of the library. The remaining three tiers of the escalator churned forward. Eli was on the fourth floor landing, stepping onto the final stretch of escalator. I hid among the students until he reached the top floor. He disappeared into the museum entrance.

On the sixth floor, in front of the glass doors to the museum, two camouflaged guards cradled assault rifles. Their faces were marked with the gruff discontent of guards everywhere in this city, just another two men who hid their fear behind guns and bulletproof vests.

When I stepped off the escalator, one of the guards tapped

the barrel of his gun against a sign indicating that I was to remove all metal objects from my pockets and place them in a plastic bin that would undergo an X-ray scan. The security check was an ad hoc, overnight installation meant to give Parisians and tourists the illusion of safety. Eli had already passed through scanner. He stood at a small desk on the other side, talking to a man checking tickets.

The guards trained their eyes on my slippers. After an hour of walking, fluff coughed out from the heels. I shrugged bashfully, like a silent comedian. My appearance upset the guards. After the attack, they viewed every rift in normalcy as a threat. I stepped forward and dropped my wallet and hotel key in the plastic bin.

The guards lifted their guns. They shouted at me in French. Their gun barrels swung from the sign to my slippers. They demanded answers for my outfit. All summer long in America police had been killing innocent people—nearly always innocent Black people—and I had, naively, considered these tragedies proof of America's uniquely wicked society. What an insidious form of exceptionalism. Terror was universal. Trigger-happy men existed all over this world, ready to sublimate fear into murder.

The guards pointed their guns at the escalator. They shouted at me again. I was to back up. I backed up. I was to leave. I was to never be heard from again, I assumed.

The scene drew Eli's attention. The guards shouted in English. "Back up!"

I pointed to the X-ray machine. My belongings had crossed

the conveyor belt and were on the other side of the metal detector. "My stuff," I whispered.

Eli approached the X-ray operator on his side of the metal detector. The man let out a chummy French laugh and snapped for the armed guards' attention. One of them swiveled his head to the operator. The other kept his rifle aimed at my heart. The operator and guard exchanged a few words. The guard shook his head. The operator made a gesture of insistence. Eli said something in French. The guard stepped to his partner and silently lowered his gun with his hand. They both looked back at Eli, who continued chatting up the X-ray operator. When he noticed them, Eli nodded and stuck up his thumb.

The guard who'd spoken to Eli beckoned me forward. He asked me a question in French. My heart was a mouse on a wheel. I couldn't capture my breath. Tired, the guard spoke in English: "You know him?" I was pardoned.

Eli mouthed, *Come on.*

I nodded at the guard. "He is my husband," I said.

With his gun, the guard made a sweeping motion toward the metal detector. He stepped aside so I could enter. Adrenaline throbbed through every pulse point on my body. I passed through the metal detector without triggering the alarm. Eli slapped the operator on the shoulder, like a grade school pal pleased to run into him so far from home.

I picked up my belongings. Eli waited for me by the ticket taker. Could it really be him? Could it be Elizabeth? "I don't have a ticket," I said.

"I bought one for you downstairs," Elizabeth said. "Let's go."

The museum was blandly enormous, as bright as a burn, the walls stretching predictably to make room for the art. Elizabeth walked ahead of me, though not with a glum sense of indifference or impatience, as I might have. She walked with the caution of a guide in the jungle. She was far more accustomed to my body than I was to hers, and I didn't mind letting her take the lead. I felt safe with her a few paces ahead, speaking to docents in French like they'd always been friends.

I had never seen myself up close in this way: freely, without the aid of a mirror, without daring my face closer to itself, to pick at my flaws. My pants fit snugly over Elizabeth's thighs and accentuated her calves, which I normally considered girthy and ugly. Elizabeth claimed to love my legs. They were sturdy, in her words. Walking behind myself, I reluctantly saw how someone might find me impressive. My gait was stern, undeterred. And the jacket added a striking severity to my shoulders. I was a handsome man. Elizabeth hadn't been lying.

"Are you coming?" she asked. Elizabeth extended my hand.

I locked her fingers with mine.

"I've been coming here every day," she said, her voice impossibly mine. "There is so much I need to show you."

"Shouldn't we talk about things?" I asked.

"Talk about what?"

"What happened to us."

"Do you really think this will be any easier if we know how it happened?" she asked. "Now come, before it gets crowded."

"It will be easier for me," I said. I wasn't sure this was true, but I felt so unmoored; an answer—even a wrong answer—might give me the grounding I needed.

Elizabeth knew better than to waste time looking for solutions that didn't exist. "I want to show you the Frankenthaler," she said.

I extracted her hand from my hand—or my hand from her hand—and followed my body through the shocking white hallways of the museum. My interest in art was more enthusiastic than learned. Elizabeth was the scholar; I was the hobbyist. When I walked through museums, I normally attached myself to the plaques next to the paintings before I let my eyes drift to the canvas, searching out the name of the painter, wondering whether I should be impressed.

Elizabeth let her eyes land where they wanted. Joining her in a museum was a scattered experience. Her parents had taught her to appreciate and to see, and she rarely noticed the names, only the paint on the canvas. She had been raised knowing beauty. Often, when the two of us stood before a piece that confounded me, she would reduce it to its most basic elements—the lines, the color, the theme—at once enhancing and puncturing my awe. "This is a middle finger to eighteenth-century portraiture," she might say, then drift away without explanation.

This day, at the Pompidou, she halted me in front of a Yves Klein sculpture, a large, textured lollipop of a sculpture painted the most perfect blue. "The point of sculpture is to defeat gravity," she said. I asked what she meant. "I told you what I meant," she replied.

In the next room, I asked whether Klein had succeeded.

"That's not for us to decide," she said, then winked, willfully cryptic.

At museums, I tried to prove myself to her, to present stark, arresting insights that would make her respect me. But every lunge I made toward knowing, every time I tried to prove to her that I *understood* a piece of art, she would topple this impulse by telling me art wasn't meant to be understood but to be felt. These were not equations. There were no clues and there were no answers. The painters spoke in color and form. What we saw were expressions that could never be articulated—it's why the painters painted.

I trailed her through the halls desperate to recognize the painters and paintings, each correct guess—the Picasso *was* a Picasso, the Matisse a Matisse—instilling me with a sense of confidence that I had been living without for ten days.

"This is the one," Elizabeth said. We stood before a tall, wide canvas hung on the wall next to the entrance to the room. "They always put her in the corner."

My back tensed hearing the anger in her voice.

It was a softly vivid abstraction featuring pools of diluted blues and pinks and greens pillowed over top of each other. I angled my head to the plaque.

Elizabeth flattened her hand over the name. "Have you already forgotten?" she asked.

"Nevelson," I ventured.

"The other one."

"Frankenthaler," I said, sure of myself.

She gave an exasperated grunt of approval and uncovered the plaque. She clasped her arms together behind her back, clutching her wrist. It was hard not to feel like a child around her in museums—where I needed the world explained for me—and today the feeling was even stronger. I was less her partner than her ward. My outfit did nothing to dispel this notion. After chasing her through the museum I could finally pause and see us how we were: Elizabeth standing with perfect posture inside my body, dressed professionally and respectable, me in her worst pair of jeans and a baggy blue sweatshirt, slippers unraveling under my ankles.

"Nevelson is a sculptor," she said. "She used reclaimed materials—wood and door handles and table legs. I know I've shown you her work. We saw it in Phoenix."

"Oh, yes I remember," I said.

"Mmhmm." She didn't believe me.

I felt as if I were deep underwater, paddling hard to the surface. "What do you like about this painting?" I asked, to divert the topic away from me.

"Isn't it obvious?"

It wasn't obvious. "You were always so drawn to blue."

"Is that your final answer?" she asked. A laugh caught in her throat. "Because there's so little blue on this canvas."

"I don't know what you want me to say."

"I used to think you weren't trying hard enough, that you were distracted when we came to museums, that you were too antsy over your phone, checking it every ten minutes, that something mundane prevented you from feeling the paintings as I felt them." She dragged a deep breath into her mouth. "But I see now it was something innate. It's a physical thing. It's something to do with this." She knocked on her chest—my chest. "It's like wearing one of those weighted vests at the dentist. Nothing gets in."

"I feel things," I said.

"The things *you* felt would buckle me. They would land me in bed for a month."

"I can't tell if you're trying to hurt me." I had never been able to tell when she got in these moods.

"What do you feel in front of this painting?"

"I like it," I said.

"That's not what I asked."

"I feel frustrated by this conversation."

"I didn't ask about this conversation. I want to know what the painting makes you feel."

A sour old man and a college-aged woman edged in beside us to stare at the canvas. They promptly moved to the Rothko spreading its wings in the center.

"I don't feel anything," I said.

"Yes, you do," she said. "But you have to focus."

Though Elizabeth rarely spent more than an hour in museums—engaging with the work deeply exhausted her—I treated museum trips like safaris. I aimed to see as many famous and popular works as I could. I cared deeply about later imposing this knowledge on others, proving to them I knew important works in important museums. Sometimes, Elizabeth would enter a museum, stand in front of a single painting, and leave after five minutes. It was maddening, and profound. It impressed me, and I loved her because she impressed me; she related to art on a level that seemed spiritual, dangerous even. The pieces she loved could ruin her day. I could never achieve such intimacy with a piece of art, and my admiration for her was weighed down by envy and despair. I wanted Elizabeth's relationship to art.

*Feel something*, I commanded myself as I stood before the Frankenthaler. I stepped closer to the canvas, but Elizabeth stuck out her arm as if I were entering traffic.

"You don't need to smell it," she said.

I tried to feel with my arms crossed, then with my hands at my hips, then with my hands clasped behind my back, the same way that Elizabeth stood, but it wasn't until, exasperated, I let my arms hang to my side that the painting came alive for me. I stepped closer again. Elizabeth didn't stop me. Perhaps I did need to smell the painting—or to feel like I could. I studied the painting in the manner that Elizabeth had taught me, years ago during a trip to the MoMA, when she advised me to notice where the colors came together or clashed, to clock the brushstrokes, to sit with the jagged, discomfiting lines, with unfinished circles, curves that straightened to spikes.

Eventually, the canvas softened around me like breath. A restless purple spreading across the base of the painting lapped into a pale mint, the green fogging over the purple in a haze that made my chest tighten. For the first time in my life, I was feeling a painting, truly feeling it, my body awash in something I could not understand. It was a disconcerting phenomenon. A large part of me wished it would end, and I angled my head to the description, but behind me Elizabeth muttered, "It will only get in the way."

The painting's washed-out tone lowered me into an Easter memory from childhood, when I was six, or seven, an Easter Sunday at my father's house when his wife was away. We spent the entire day biting the ears off chocolate rabbits and stuffing marshmallow Peeps in our mouths, sucking yellow crystals from our fingers before plucking out more Peeps from the carton. This memory wasn't merely a memory; it was happiness, a rare moment of joy I shared with my father, a moment of hope, for in that day was the promise of similar days, hope that this man I gullibly loved would stop treating me like a customer filing complaints when I visited his apartment. I was not prepared to feel this way. Not in public. Not in front of Elizabeth. I sat down at a padded bench in the center of the room to collect myself.

The older man and his young girlfriend, or student, or

daughter, were sitting on the bench, but they stood when I settled next to them. I was not a safe or comforting presence in my outfit, and they were right to shuttle away.

Elizabeth took the open space beside me and lowered her hand to my wrist. "When I lived here, in college," she said. "I told you about that, didn't I?"

Of course she had. It hurt to be asked.

"I used to come here every weekend to see this painting. It was the fall semester, and every day the days were pinching shut a little bit tighter, fall dragging a dark sheet over the city, and I was desperate for color that might tear me away from life in the library and the dorms. Those were the darkest months of my life. This painting saved my life. I owe it so much."

"You never told me you were so depressed when you lived here."

"It embarrassed me. Such a cliché. Sad American girl on a study abroad trip."

Such a soft and simple thing, sadness, and she treated it like a monster. I considered telling her she had no reason to feel ashamed of her sadness—but Elizabeth knew this, and she bristled at anything close to condescension, so I kept this reassurance to myself, convinced it would only offend her.

"Why are you telling me now?" I asked.

"It all feels far away," she said.

"It's been a decade," I said.

"That's not at all what I mean."

"I get it," I said, though we both knew I didn't and never would.

"I woke up here," she said.

"In the Pompidou?"

"In the hotel where we're staying. It used to be owned by my college—it was an alumni building, and they housed us there for our study abroad. But they sold the property after 2008."

"Who's paying for the room?"

"I'm staying until they tell me I can't any longer. I don't really care who's paying—maybe I'm paying, maybe you are, maybe some extraterrestrial being is paying, or God is paying, or whatever sorcerer made this happen to us—but there's no use in asking that question." It was just like Elizabeth to glibly glide between self-worth and indifference. She deserved this hotel, and she deserved not to waste any time wondering how the room came into her possession—that was a question for some other time, for some other person, for someone who cared about trivial details.

I felt stupid for even asking the question.

"I'm here because of this painting," she said. "You felt it, didn't you?"

"You mean was I moved?" I asked, without trying to hide my defensiveness. "I thought that was the point—to feel something. That's what you keep telling me. It's what you're always telling me."

"I mean differently than you felt before. I saw you. You weren't hunting out the curator's description or the year it was finished. You experienced it. It took you someplace."

My defenses lowered. Her words—always so deftly selected—could spotlight parts of me I hadn't known were apparent. I was so obvious to her. I nodded, as if confessing a secret.

"I've been coming here every day since I woke up in Paris," she said.

"No wonder you're so friendly with the guards."

"I'm a friendly person," she said. Then, bitterly, "It's even easier now to be friendly."

"What's that supposed to mean?"

"If you don't know, there's no point in explaining it."

"You always underestimated your capacity for cruelty."

"No, I didn't," she said.

I stood in protest but had nowhere to go. Elizabeth waited for me to realize this, and when I returned to my seat, she continued speaking like nothing had happened.

"Do you see that painting over there?" she asked. "The red abstraction front and center so no one will miss it?"

The young woman and grim older man stood in front of it now, mumbling respectfully. I squinted to make out the name of the painter.

"Who doesn't matter," Elizabeth said. "What matters is that it's a piece of shit. I doubt the artist was capable of holding a paintbrush—his assistants probably painted it for him, based on some half-cooked idea he fed to them from his *genius* mouth." No one ever said *genius* with more anger. "There's no eye for color, so he relies on reds and texture. You see the brushstrokes? He's trying to make something dull appear powerful but he failed."

"Those people seem to like it," I said.

"Trust me," she said. "He failed. He likely chose red because of a dream he had—the most prevalent and noxious excuse for bad art. The greatest travesty, though, is that the piece is completely stripped of feeling; it's nothing more than a label affixed to a can. It's a work of pure narcissism, the kind of dribble an artist produces once they believe they're a genius—once they start believing what people say about their work."

Part of me wanted to dismiss her remarks as callous, or bitter, or signs of personal preference, but her intelligence mesmerized me. For three years, I had taken her statements as dogma. Elizabeth was smarter than me, more accomplished; what use was there in thinking for myself when she made the truth so abundantly clear? I nudged closer to her, so our shoulders touched. Her intelligence turned me on, as much now as before The Incident.

"Do you like what's happened to us?" she asked.

"I can't possibly answer that," I said, which I intended to mean that there was no answer for such a question, that this wasn't something you could like or dislike, but the truth was I hadn't thought about whether I liked it or not. I moved through life like an airplane through clouds.

"I can't name a single thing I don't like about it," she said. "Everything's become so much easier for me in your body."

"You sound like a cliché of feminism," I said.

"What do you know about feminism?" she asked.

"Only what you told me," I said. It was too true of a statement not to be funny. Elizabeth let out a deep, spirited laugh, the kind that came from the pit of my throat. "Does this mean you don't love me anymore?"

"Why wouldn't I love you?"

"It sounds like you don't want to go back."

"You're always so drastic," she said. "If I didn't love you I'd try to change back." She laughed again, but this time it was unmistakably hers, a slim blade of a laugh, confident and disarming. I loved that laugh and loved it even more coming from me. "This is the ultimate act of love, Eli, inhabiting you, living as you, *shitting* as you. To fully inhabit your body and not run away. There's no way to love anyone more."

"I hadn't thought about it that way," I admitted.

"How else could you possibly think about it?"

"My mom has been calling me, insisting that I come find you. I don't know how to talk about it most days. Everyone in Bulgaria thinks that you—thinks that I left you, that I abandoned you in a foreign country."

"That is what happened," she said. "That is absolutely what happened."

"You used her credit card," I said. "You must have known she'd find you."

"I knew she would buy you a ticket if she thought you were here."

"Why wouldn't you write to me?"

"This is all too strange and too fun to risk with direct communication."

"Nothing about this is fun," I said.

"Have you tried touching me yet?" she asked.

Just once, by accident in the shower. "I haven't," I said.

"That's a shame," she said. "I can't get enough of your dick."

I shushed her. "We're in a museum," I whispered.

"This place is loaded with dicks," she said. "There's no better place to talk about dicks."

"It seemed skeevy to touch you, like some middle-aged man's fantasy come to life."

"You never did like my body as much as I liked yours."

"You're very beautiful," I said.

"I never said I wasn't," she said. "We're both very good-looking. We're an attractive couple, though I am, objectively speaking, better looking than you are, and that's a shame for me, because that never seemed to matter to you."

"Beauty isn't everything," I said.

"Please," she said. "We're in a museum."

"Maybe I'm asexual," I said. In past relationships, I'd always been the first to quit initiating sex, the first to choose nights lounging lustlessly watching TV over repeated fits in the bedroom.

"Sometimes I hold on to you when I'm bored," she said. "It used to never make sense, when I'd catch you clutching yourself. But it's like a stress ball. Something you squeeze to allay your anxiety."

"Please don't use it like that," I said.

"I'm not so unimaginative," she said. "Trust me: I really do love your dick. It's an excellent one."

"So I guess you've seen them all?" It was a rare spit of anger from me.

"Please let me compliment you for once without putting one of us down."

I apologized. I wanted her to return to the painting, for her to tell me more about Frankenthaler and the sexism she faced from the industry; I wanted to hear Elizabeth tell me how *her* writing career paralleled the painter's career, how both of them faced unrealistic demands from an artistic community that privileged male mediocrity. I went so far as to ask: "How difficult was it for Frankenthaler to show her work as a woman?"

"Not hard at all," Elizabeth said. "She was a rich girl. Wealthy from birth. That makes everything easy. A brilliant rich girl, no doubt. But rich nonetheless." She slid her hand up my knees to my thigh, her middle finger riding the inseam to my crotch.

"What are you doing?"

"Why do you think I brought you here?" She tucked her thumb in my front pocket and swept her fingers to my ass. The shock of my hand on her body made me shudder. I felt myself getting wet, the sensation peculiar and thrilling, like breaking through the surface of a lake.

"Here?" I asked.

"There's a bathroom nearby, and it's always empty. Even emptier today." She extracted her hands from my pockets and clasped onto my finger, guiding me into a stand and then into the next room, and the next, the painting and sculptures and video clips and the chairs were all dull splashes of color and noise compared with the urgency of holding Elizabeth's hand, trailing her, silently as a snail, through the afterlife white of the museum hallways, until she turned a corner toward the restrooms. We passed the women's room. We paused at the men's. A yellow sign hung above the handle.

"It's out of order," I said.

"Not for what we're doing."

Elizabeth locked the door behind us.


MY FORAYS INTO BISEXUALITY WERE BRIEF AND FRACTURED: the occasional kiss, the grab of a crotch through thick jeans, hands inexpertly grazing, often driven by curiosity more than arousal. In the bathroom, though, I felt an unadulterated excitement.

"Kiss me," Elizabeth said. She leaned me back against the marble counter between the two middle sink basins and kissed me harder than I'd ever been kissed. She didn't normally use tongue, but she pressed hers into my mouth with the intensity of a dog lapping up water.

"You're so aggressive," I said.

"You never fuck me," she said.

She pushed me against the sink so the corner dug into the flesh at the tops of my hamstrings. Her hands clutched my hips, then a single finger rose up my spine to my neck. After three years together, we had settled into a successful sexual routine that guaranteed orgasms, as efficient as a pit crew changing a tire. Now, neither of us knew how to act in our bodies—bodies we both believed we had mastered—and I sensed Elizabeth groping, literally, for signs of how to please me under these new conditions.

It was our first time all over again. She tugged my hair and bit my bottom lip, drawing it toward her like taffy. Dribbles of blood coppered our tongues. She scooped her hands under my ass and hefted me onto the counter with an ease that seemed to surprise her.

"I'm lighter than I thought," she said.

"Or I'm stronger," I said. I wrapped my legs around Elizabeth's waist and wrenched her against me so I could feel her cock on my thigh. I'd never felt someone hard against me. I tightened my legs to press her cock even closer. She wrenched my ass in response, kissed me tonguefully, while I slid the suit jacket down her shoulders. She shook the jacket to the floor. I unbuttoned her top two buttons but paused to let her tug my sweatshirt over my head.

In many ways, I was a sexual simpleton. I enjoyed missionary and hand jobs and head. I came with staggering—frustrating—ease. Normally, I got Elizabeth off using my hands before we moved to my needs. It was better this way. It guaranteed sexual equity. Had nothing happened to us, had we been ourselves in this bathroom, I would have patiently rubbed her asshole and clit until she came with shattering moans, but I was eager to please myself.

I unzipped Elizabeth's pants and dipped my hand inside to the wrist. Her button was still buttoned, her belt still buckled, and I couldn't get a good hold on her cock. She unbuttoned her pants and clattered the buckle until it came loose.

"Just take them off," she said. She liked to get naked as soon as we agreed to fuck, a habit I found unsettling—I hated to be naked, a habit, no doubt, that unsettled her.

Her pants and underwear bunched at her ankles; her cock stuck out like a plank. The first cock that would fuck me was mine. I stifled a laugh and slid off the counter, spun us around so I could see Elizabeth's face in the mirror. Seeing her straining and messy-haired turned me on, just as it had when I'd been in my body. She unbuttoned my jeans and inched them to my calves. I sank to the floor and kissed the tip of her cock. It was girthy, about the length of a TV remote. It would be fairly easy to take.

"Is this weird for you?" Elizabeth asked. She was staring down at me.

"Of course it's weird for me," I said.

"Just making sure." She ran her fingers through my hair, palmed the back of my skull.

I tried to fit everything in my mouth and nipped the base of her cock.

"Yow!" She flinched.

I gagged her out of me, a string of spittle binding her to my bottom lip.

"There's no rush," she said. Of course there was a rush! We were fucking in a public restroom. The point of fucking here was rushing, the rush. A docent or guard would soon test their hand on the door after seeing us enter the alcove for the restrooms. Someone would become suspicious if we didn't emerge very soon.

I drew my tongue up the shaft of Elizabeth's cock, a move she excelled at, though I avoided her balls because her mouth on my balls made me uncomfortable, though I never had the heart to tell her. I swiped up the left side of her cock, base to tip, then down the right side, tip to base, and when I put her back in my mouth I lifted my eyes to meet Elizabeth's. Her face held a look of self-satisfaction. Not pleasure, exactly, but not not pleasure.

"Keep looking at me," she said. I would've felt like a misogynist for saying this to her, but I loved hearing it, as if it were the voice of my own desire cleansed of all inhibitions. A chill spread through my back. I inhaled the ruddy scent of myself.

I returned her to my mouth without gagging, acclimating myself to this situation, asserting and retreating as she let out bearish grunts of approval. I faked a moan how Elizabeth moaned because it normally helped me, but the fake moans became real. I began to want things, or to accept that I wanted things, and I couldn't tell if what I wanted were things I had always wanted but had never acknowledged or if they were things I wanted only because I was in Elizabeth's body. "Pull my hair," I mumbled. She twisted her fingers in my hair and tugged it gently, until I said "harder," and she yanked like she might rip the hair from my scalp. I moaned even louder from the pain and slipped her deeper into my mouth and then out a few times before jacking her off.

We knew so intimately what the other was feeling. When Elizabeth's thighs started to tremble, I moaned even louder to let her know I wanted her, and she must've known that my moans were as much for her as for me.

"I think I'm gonna come," she said.

I knew she was. Her thighs tensed to telephone poles. I told her to come in my mouth and readied my lips at the tip of her cock as I jacked her off. It was easier this way, we knew.

"Fuck, fuck, fuck," she said. Warmth leaked softly into the back of my throat, little guttural sprays of heat that continued unabated for what felt like minutes. It tasted like hot, saltwater yogurt and pooled selfishly in the dip of my tongue. She quivered inside me. I gulped, looking up at her, but her eyes were pinched shut in pleasure, hand clasping the back of my head.

When it was over, she opened her eyes. Her hands were on my shoulders, then under my arms. She lifted me to her and angled her body away from the sink to make room for me to spit out her cum. I told her I didn't need that.

"You know I don't swallow," she said.

"You're not you anymore," I replied.

"Turn around," she said.

We positioned ourselves so that I was closest to the mirror. The counter rose as high as our waists, so the mirror cut off at the first hints of flesh and pubic hair. Elizabeth guided her hand between me and the counter to play with my clit, rubbing in experienced circles that lit every light in my body. Had I rubbed her clit the same way? Using this particular motion? I couldn't remember, and my forgetfulness carried me out of my body, away from the pleasure I wanted to feel.

Sex had always been a source of anxiety for me. I fretted

over the usual things: performance, pleasure, duration. But our circumstances only heightened my anxiety. Every touch seemed like a lesson in how she truly wished to be touched. Her hands were signs I'd done everything wrong.

She pressed her cock into the flesh of my ass. She was still hard but softening quickly and I knew she wanted to fuck. Two fingers entered me. Then a third. I let out a quivering gasp, and the gasp spread to the tips of my fingers and toes.

Elizabeth removed her fingers and tilted me flatter against the counter, bending her knees for a better angle. She drove the tip forward, filling me with her, and I curled my left hand around the faucet for leverage and flattened my other hand in the bowl of the sink. I'd been averting my eyes from the mirror, unwilling to look at myself, but as Elizabeth fucked me I lifted my head. It was so very mundane. What I saw was no different from us fucking in front of a mirror in the apartment we'd shared in Arizona, no different from the few times we'd fucked in the shower in Bulgaria. All that had changed was perspective.

Elizabeth sensed herself getting soft and fucked faster to make me come before she had nothing left. I had no expectation of coming, not in this body, which she insisted was a supremely difficult body for achieving orgasm, a statement I had taken for granted over three years together but had never doubted, until now, wondering whether it had been said and said and said and said not out of truth but to protect my self-esteem.

"Are you close?" she asked.

"How would I know?"

She pulled my hair and sped up. I pressed my palms against the mirror and drew my face close to the glass, fogging it with frantic breaths. She slapped my right ass cheek. I thrust myself against her in rhythm.

"I'm close," I said, because I very well may have been.

She draped herself over my back. She bit the rim of my ear and tongued the inside. Her hands explored my body with purpose and confusion and desperation. One hand held my tits; the other returned to my clit.

"Keep going," I said. "That's it, right there." And that *was* it. My breath galloped like a horse fleeing its pen. I moved my right hand so it covered my face—Eli's face—in the mirror, and she brought the hand that had been up my shirt to the mirror, covering Elizabeth's reflection. Sensation spread even farther through me, as if trying to launch out of my body.

Elizabeth had hardened again, a miracle in the city of lights. She moved her hands to my hips, fucking me as hard as she could, impatiently enthusiastic, exhausted.

"You're gonna come," I said.

"Again?" she said.

"Pull out," I said.

"Are you gonna come?"

"I might have," I said.

"I want to come in you," she said.

I wanted that too. She kept fucking me, and I kept feeling and feeling, the feeling becoming more of itself, until it was tingling everywhere over my body, and inside my body, where the warmth of myself was traveling through me. I was coming. She had come. Warm liquid dribbled down between my thighs. I turned around, hooked my arms under her armpits. We kissed. Tender but tongueless.

"Do you love me?" she asked.

"What kind of question is that?"

# PART IV

Elizabeth never considered herself the marrying type. As a girl, she'd imagined adulthood full of lovers and accolades, a Simone de Beauvoir type of life, obtaining and discarding the Sartres and Algrens and Camuses of her generation between writing radical treatises that undermined bourgeois conventions. She intended to be free.

Then the fellowship email arrived. *Congratulations! We are writing to award you* etc. After reading it, Elizabeth felt: *I do not want to live overseas by myself.* She and Eli consulted. Eli had nowhere to be. He'd wanted to quit the restaurant for years. She responded, asking whether her partner could join and was told that yes, he could, but there would be no additional funding for her husband.

ALL HER LIFE SHE HAD LONGED FOR THE VERY THINGS THE fellowship promised her: travel, sex, freedom, acclaim. Should she really bring a husband into that world?

ELI WAS A PATIENT AND CONFIDENT LOVER, FUNNY—ALBEIT undependable—and willing to admit when he'd wronged her, a rare trait compared with the other men she'd dated and loved. Even after cheating on her—the memory of which still made her feel brittle with self-loathing and shame—he had acted with genuine remorse and had not, as far as she could tell, done anything similar since. He was willing to change. And he knew her. He could tell when she was angry, when she was depressed, and he knew the appropriate reactions to her feelings, when to fracture her mood with a joke, when to allow her the space. Jesus. He *knew* her. He was, she feared, the first man who ever had.

BUT THEY'D KNOWN EACH OTHER ONLY THREE YEARS. SHE'D owned flip-flops for longer. Goldfish had lengthier life spans. Flies, probably.

HER TASTE, HOWEVER, HAD BEEN VALIDATED, AND SHE loved having been proved right. In their three years together, he'd published a handful of small stories in even smaller magazines, more than some of her peers in The Program, and she liked having chosen the man, of all the men available to her, willing to work harder than the others.

BUT DID SHE REALLY WANT TO BECOME ONE OF THOSE people who married after graduate school? Online, there were others. Enemies from high school. Friends from Hinneman. Other writers at other Programs, lofting their printed theses, diamonds glinged on their fingers. How bad had the world become that even the artists were getting engaged?

IT WASN'T THAT SHE DIDN'T WANT TO LIVE OVERSEAS ALONE. She didn't want to spend a year away from Eli. His fingers. His ears. His tongue. His mouth. His hair. His cock. His ass. His calves. His elbows. His biceps. His hands. His hands on the scoop of her back. His hands on her ass. His hands gliding her inner thighs.

THE STATE OF ARIZONA DID NOT WANT ANYONE GOING unwed. They waited in line for an hour at the county clerk's office alongside the marrying and the divorcing and the name-changing and the soon-to-be-voting. Once their number was called, they passed their IDs to the clerk and confirmed their names were correctly spelled. They were given forms to complete and return.

She waited until after receiving the forms—once it seemed official—to deliver the news to her parents. Her parents had had an elaborate wedding, hosting hundreds of family members and friends of friends to fulfill their parents' desires. They told Elizabeth many times how much they resented their parents for putting them through that charade—they would have preferred something simple, a rejection of their lavish upbringings—and she felt insulated from judgment by their shared stance against hypocrisy. They were not, in the end, alarmed when Elizabeth told them she planned to marry Eli. They liked Eli and nothing they said would change her mind, even if they found her decision hasty and mildly delusional, which they did.

HER PARENTS WOULDN'T BE ABLE TO JOIN THEM, NOR COULD her closest childhood friends, not under short notice. Most of her friends believed that she was lying. Elizabeth, they thought, couldn't possibly be the first one among them to marry. Some might have been able to make it but refused to travel simply for fear of falling victim to an elaborate practical joke.

If Elizabeth had to marry in Arizona, away from her family and friends, then she wanted to take advantage of what Arizona could offer. She would marry in the desert surrounded by twelve people free on a Tuesday at 2:00. A friend of Eli's, the bartender he'd gone to the sports bar to visit the night he and Elizabeth met, offered to guide them into the desert. He'd lived here his whole life. He would find them someplace lovely to marry. The Pathfinder, Elizabeth called him. The other guests were given roles and titles as well, to ensure their commitment: The Minister, The Oracle, The Ring Bearer, The Mentors, The Screamers, The Guards, The Historian, and The DJ.

THE PATHFINDER STOPPED HIS CAR NEAR AN EMPTY PATCH of desert an hour west of the university. He got out, started to walk, and they followed. It was unclear whose property it was—public or private—and when they exited their cars, they were greeted by the sounds of four-wheelers revving and shotguns firing, though the drivers were too far away to see, imbuing the noises with a sense of permanence, as if it were wind they were hearing. "They shouldn't be here either," The Pathfinder said. "No one will bother us."

Cactuses tined high into the sky. Brush blundered under their feet, and they stepped over it cautiously, careful to leave the land as they found it. Damaging a saguaro in Arizona could land you in prison. Kicking innocent brush would likely result in a fine they couldn't afford.

Elizabeth wore a breezy sage dress that pooled around gladiator sandals and a dignified layer of makeup. Eli was the one to wear white: a snowy button-down split by a bolo tie that belonged to Elizabeth; his pants were brown, pleasantly plaid, and they accentuated his ass—she loved seeing him in these pants.

"HERE," THE PATHFINDER SAID AT THE FOOT OF A SMALL hill. The ceremony commenced.

The Oracle passed out scraps of paper and golf pencils to each guest and advised everyone to write down their sins. The Oracle dug a small hole in the earth with his hands. Once the sins were inscribed, the papers were placed in the hole and covered with dirt. The Oracle blessed the guests. Their sins were absolved.

The Mentors split everyone in two lines. Each Mentor stood at the head of one line and gave a brief speech about the importance of trust in a marriage. The guests second in line turned their backs to The Mentors. "Close your eyes," said The Mentors. "And fall into my arms." Elizabeth and Eli went last. Afterward, they took turns falling into each other's chest.

The Screamers demanded everyone scream. Everyone screamed. The screaming portion concluded.

The Guards kept an eye out for intruders.

The Historian took photos for Instagram.

The DJ blasted a playlist called "Fun Wedding Hits" on his phone.

The Minister called the couple together at the foot of a cactus. At its crown, a pair of hawks peered down from their nest, silently staring in approval, Elizabeth believed.

The Ring Bearer emerged from the brush cupping the rings in his hands like a small, delicate sun. The rings were from a supermarket vending machine and were plastic and garish, little spinny things strapped on the tops.

Eli read to Elizabeth from his book about butlers. "We might be nothing," he said after finishing, "but at least we'll be nothing together."

Elizabeth read from a popular feminist book about how men explained things to women, explaining to Eli why he must never explain things to her, if he planned on loving her.

The Minister encouraged a kiss.

It was chaste, at first, but as the guests started to cheer, Eli lowered his arm to the small of Elizabeth's back, preparing to dip her. He loved the attention, and she loved his impulse to entertain—she rarely let herself show off like this—and as her back tilted, hair spilling free to the dirt, she felt small for the first time since she was a child, vulnerable and protected and held, safe even as her body humbled close to the earth, because his arm was underneath her, and his mouth was on hers, and even as she spied one of the hawks fleeing its nest, she was sure this wasn't an omen, that the only omen worth trusting was the two hawks in the nest, that it meant nothing for them to leave, because they *had* been there, they had watched over them, they had approved, and when it was time, she held on to Eli as he lifted her into a stand, exactly where she needed to be.

Outside, sitting on the angled ground of the plaza, Elizabeth lectured me on her body's needs and demands, like a parent checking off rules for a babysitter. Despite my effort to keep up appearances, there was so much I hadn't considered. Her fingernails were entirely too long and her face, according to her, was offensively dry. "Have you spotted yet?" she asked. "Spotted?" I said. "Jesus," she said. "There are pads under the sink," she said. "I know where they are," I said, a hopeless recovery. She gave me detailed instructions for how to peel off the adhesive covering and attach the pad to the thin bridge of her underwear. Her attention to detail disheartened me. Did she really think I couldn't figure this out for myself?

She stood, then lowered her hand to lift me up. We walked to a packed patisserie. Beneath rose gold lighting, a glitzy display of macarons stretched the length of the room. The women behind the counter took requests with unflusterable grace. They boxed orders into elaborate cardboard containers fit to carry Fabergé eggs. The machinery of the patisserie mesmerized me.

The women boxed the macarons the way angels would, each woman thinner and prettier than the last, a line of beauty intensifying into absence.

Elizabeth told me to decide what I wanted before we reached the front of the line. We wouldn't have any time to decide once we got there. But I couldn't look away from the women. I watched them with something like desire that wasn't exactly desire—rather, it was a new form of desire, one I didn't quite know how to manage. My eyes drifted away from their mouths and their breasts and their asses to the black liner winging out from their eyes, to the belts on their high-waisted skirts, the bracelets ringing their wrists and the rings rounding their fingers. I imagined wearing their jewelry, my hair flawlessly pinned, gliding behind the counter with the same effortless charm—I'd never wanted anything more than to be what these women were.

"What do you want?" Elizabeth asked, once we reached the front of the line.

I confessed I hadn't been thinking about the macarons.

The cashier flicked her right hand in a simple sweep toward the door. She called for the next person. I stepped back and gazed at the display, assuming the next available cashier would attend to us, but Elizabeth tugged gently at my elbow and guided me to the end of the line. I couldn't look at her, worried she was angry at me for losing our spot. She whispered, "It took me four tries the first time I came in here. No doubt we can do better than that." At the end of the line, she wrapped her fingers over my palm, mitten-like, the way she preferred—like a parent and child crossing the street. The line burned down like a fuse.

"The pistachio is excellent," she said. "And I've been loving the raspberry too. But you can't go wrong with any of them." She had an entire life in this city.

I looked at our hands. We appeared entirely ordinary. A straight couple holding hands in line waiting for macarons. We were treating ourselves to an afternoon snack. Sure, my hair was messy from sex, but in Paris everyone's hair is either perfect or messy from sex, and it was a privilege to join with the latter so early in the day.

"Be ready this time," she said. "I don't want to have to go back again."

The problem with loving someone at their best is seeing them at their worst. Elizabeth, capable of such generosity, of skin-diminishing empathy, could just as easily slip into pettiness and malice when burdened.

At the front of the line, Elizabeth spoke to the cashier in French, and the woman folded a plastic rectangle into a box. The woman peered impatiently at me. I asked Elizabeth to order first. She ordered the pistachio and the raspberry, the only two flavors that had entered my mind. They both turned their gazes to me.

I pointed nervously at a brown macaron, some variety of chocolate, and the cashier pinched rubber-gloved fingers around my selection and removed it like a surgeon extracting a lung. The macaron took its place in the box. I pointed at a yellow one—lemon, I imagine—and everyone inside the patisserie sighed. The cashier gently dented it as she removed it from the display. The macaron was tossed in the trash.

Elizabeth intervened. There would be no lemon in our box. She ordered a rose macaron from the end of the display, and it was, somehow, my turn again. "That one," I said, and pressed my finger to the glass over a row of purple macarons.

"Lavender," said the cashier. "Excellent choice." She gave me a look both sympathetic and damning, the type of look from which most people never recover. Elizabeth paid.

WE ATE THE MACARONS ON A BENCH BACK IN THE PLAZA. The bubble man dragged his wand through the air, and I feared one of the parents from earlier might recognize me. But hours had passed. The children and parents had been replaced by new children and parents.

"I don't normally wear makeup," Elizabeth said. "But you'll find liquid foundation, lipstick, and mascara in a black zipper bag next to the sink. You won't need anything more."

"I know where it is," I told her.

"Very good," she said.

I expected her to ask if I'd tried putting it on; when she didn't, I told her I had.

"How did it look?" she asked.

"Don't you want to ask why I was wearing it?"

"I will when I'm ready," she said. She attempted a delicate bite of the pistachio but it collapsed at the touch of her teeth. Crumbs flecked into her lap.

"I watched a tutorial showing me how to apply it," I said.

"I don't know why I never tried that."

"It wasn't something you cared about."

"I know what I cared about," she said, somehow without a hint of resentment. "I cared deeply about looking good. But it's something you never wanted to notice about me."

"I thought you looked good."

"No you didn't."

"No one looks good all the time," I said.

"I'm embarrassed by how badly I wanted you to tell me I was beautiful, that I was hot, for you to want me." She placed a macaron in my hand, the brown one that I'd selected first. "Do you know how hard it is to want someone to call you pretty? Do you think I liked wanting something so simple and dumb?"

"I assumed you were above wanting to hear all those things."

"No woman is above that," she said. "Never truly above it. Some hide it better than others but it's impossible not to care, to never truly care."

"I'm sorry," I said.

"For what?" she asked.

I was ashamed of neglecting her—I was always missing the things that were right in front of me. I ate my chocolate macaron before taking a teensy bite of the raspberry. The bubble man summoned a bubble the size of the moon. The children galloped and jumped, their sticky hands clapping at suds. Elizabeth ate the remains of the raspberry in one wolfish bite, then dragged her forearm across her face to loosen the crumbs stuck to her lips.

"You know where all the teaching supplies are, right?"

"You expect me to go back to teaching?"

"This is a great opportunity for you," she said.

"It's your opportunity."

"Consider it my gift to you: My accomplishments are now yours. Do with them whatever you like."

"You're not making sense," I said.

"What about any of this makes the slightest bit of sense?"

"I don't want your job. I don't want your life."

"Neither of us has much of a choice in the matter."

"Your parents flew out to Sofia to see you," I said. She loved her parents deeply, and, since we arrived, she'd been longing to see them. Did she really want to abandon them?

She took a minute registering my comment. She brought her hand to her chin and tapped a single finger against her cheek, where, as I anticipated, she hadn't taken the time to shave. "What have you told them?" she asked.

"I told them what everyone else already assumed: that I've been left by my husband."

"Promise me you won't let them put me in an institution."

"That's an impossible promise," I said, half-joking.

She said nothing.

I promised.

"I've worked too hard to waste my life on a twin mattress, playing card games and going to group for eight hours a day. I need you to be okay in front of everyone."

"I'm handling all of this very well," I said. "Considering."

"You're wearing hotel slippers," she said.

"Just tell me what I need to know."

"You're a smart person," she said. "You're more than capable of figuring all of this out for yourself." She stood. Without turning toward me she said, "I did." She started in the direction of the hotel.

I stood but immediately sat back down; in moments like this Elizabeth did not like to be followed. She valued her privacy after fights and would spend those hours drifting around the neighborhood on walks, her anger cooling like a stone in the snow. Before she got far, however, she shouted, "Are you coming?"

I trotted over.

"Why didn't you follow me?" she asked.

"You seemed like you wanted space."

"You're the one who always needed space."

"I forgot the macarons," I said.

"We don't need them," she said. After a few minutes walking in silence, she said, "Tell your mother you couldn't find me."

"My mother as in my mother? And you as in me?"

"Whatever way ends with you telling Eli's mother that Eli is missing. You looked everywhere. You tried your best. And now you fear the worst."

"She'll never believe that."

"Were you not here on Friday?"

"People actually died," I said. "Real people."

"I'm a real person," she said.

For the first time, I could see how the qualities in Elizabeth that so impressed me—her relentlessness, her intelligence, the precision of the stories she told—could also make me uneasy. I had known for some time that my best qualities were also my worst. I was fun, thus irresponsible; charming and manipulative; loving made me prone to resentment; my intelligence skirted close to connivance. She was capable of the same callousness and opportunism that I had, naively, reserved only for myself, and recognizing it then made me shudder with affection. She had no idea what to do. She was confused, and her vulnerability—a word she never would have used to describe herself in that moment—made me want to fix this for her.

I always trusted Elizabeth. There was no point in arguing with her when she made up her mind. But she hadn't made up her mind. I could tell she didn't like taking advantage of the attack any more than I did; she simply couldn't imagine other options. "Suicide," I said.

"You'd be okay with that?" she asked. "With how it would—for your mom?"

"It wouldn't surprise her, I don't think." My entire body felt heavy with honesty.

Elizabeth slipped her fingers around mine, and we paused, taking in what we were doing. We said nothing for a few minutes, standing smack on the sidewalk as passersby circled us. She appeared to reconsider her plan, recognizing the pain it would cause (to my mom, to her family, to both of us), and I gazed at her lips—my own chapped, familiar lips—waiting for her to walk everything back. "Won't you miss me?" she asked.

"I already miss you."

"Then talk me out of it."

"I know by now when I can and cannot talk you out of something."

She said nothing.

So I tried to talk her out of it. Eventually, we would likely change back, and when that happened I wouldn't want to continue however she'd decided to live her life. Didn't she long to see her parents again? We shouldn't use tragedy for our personal gain—the dead deserved so much more. My mother didn't deserve to senselessly grieve. *We* didn't deserve to grieve. We were young and we were in love and wasn't that reason enough?

"I'm sorry," she said. "But my mind is already made up. I didn't think I would enjoy this as much as I do. But it's intoxicating."

"Do you even miss me?"

"I still love you, and I always will. You're my favorite person. But I'm no longer sure that I need you. This might be our best opportunity to live lives more suited to our abilities."

"What you're saying doesn't make any sense."

"We both knew it would happen this way," she said. "That you would leave me."

"You're the one who has all the accolades."

"That's what I'm saying. It's been this way from the start. You move into *my* apartment, and you're the one who cheats on me."

"That was a mistake."

"It was a pattern—but one I accepted, because, despite everything, I love you, I really do. And that's the most frustrating part of all of this. Because I do so much for you, I do everything, and you never seem to appreciate it. I have been everything for you."

For every couple, there is one argument from which all others emerge. This was ours: I was ungrateful, I never gave her as much as she gave me. And she was right. I took from her; I took from so many people. The boys I emulated; the strangers I sprayed with invasive personal stories; my mom, whom I'd exposed in the stories I wrote during college. But that didn't mean I had to agree with Elizabeth. "You act like you're better than me."

"Because I am better than you. I'm smarter than you, I'm kinder than you, I'm more talented and better looking. And you benefit from *all* of that. It's exhausting. And I want to benefit. Things should be easy for me."

It didn't hurt to hear her say those things. I felt the same way. "Fine," I said. "But I'm not telling my mother I'm dead."

"Fair enough," she said. "Tell her you noticed a backpack went missing and a few days' worth of clothes. Tell her I took a train to Paris—I left after you went to school in the morning."

"But you weren't going to school in the morning."

"Then I left after lunch."

"You never go out for lunch on your own."

"I don't know, then. You figure it out."

"I don't like this," I said.

"You will," she said. "You're getting everything that you want, okay. You're getting a writing career and a fellowship and a family that cares about you."

"My mom isn't a deadbeat."

"And the attention you crave," she added. According to her, I was desperate for pity and sympathy, and I would receive it in spades if I returned to Bulgaria single.

"I had a difficult childhood," I said.

"No one is disputing that," she said. "No one's saying you don't deserve the attention. Like I said, this is my gift to you. You get everything that I accomplished."

"Life isn't so much easier for me."

"Let's not wade into hypotheticals," she said. "I know for a fact it's easier for you."

Elizabeth had been planning her escape since she woke up in Paris. It pained me to learn she hadn't spent the time looking for me but had instead strategized ways to avoid me forever. "You didn't come looking for me either," she said. "Maybe you loved being me."

There had been something thrilling about the way people treated me. They pitied me, sure, but they also admired me. Her teaching mentor yelled because she expected better from Elizabeth. Desi and Kiril looked at me with cold respect rather than chummy condescension. There had even been an email from a literary agent, and though I hadn't responded, I read and reread the effusive letter as if it really *were* my work the agent was praising. Elizabeth could be cruel and exacting. But she was rarely, if ever, wrong.

"What if you get found out?" I asked.

"If that happens, then I'll return to our old life. I'll say I had a dissociative episode. People love those kinds of stories—you did, after all, have a traumatic childhood. It's not beyond the realm of possibilities. Your mental health has never been one hundred percent."

"How kind of you to say."

"You know that's the type of thing that I like." She stretched to kiss me on the cheek.

On lazy weekend afternoons, we liked playing a game called Could You Date? *Could you date an accountant?* one of us would ask, and then we'd list all the reasons why we couldn't. *Could you date someone with a trust fund? Could you date a mechanical engineer?* In this way, we created a list of all the things we liked about each other through the things we couldn't stand about imagined lovers. For two people who spent their lives writing and addressing their feelings, we should've been better at articulating what we loved about each other. It was as if language were not a means to capture truth but to conceal it. We skated around the edges of truth without ever slipping inside.

"So it's decided?" I asked.

"For the time being," she said. "But I might change my mind. I like to remain open to anything."

"Including disassociation."

"Don't pretend this isn't difficult for me too. I'm going to miss my parents. I'll miss my life. I'll miss going home."

"You'll miss me."

"I already miss you so much," she said. "You don't need to be insecure about that. This has nothing to do with how much I miss you."

"When does it begin?" I asked. "When do you start your new life?"

"You're really not going to say it?"

I didn't want to. I was angry with her. "I miss you too," I said.

"Good." She kissed me goodbye.

At 8:47 p.m., I knocked on the door of hotel room 847. The patterns man answered immediately, dressed in the same robe I wore in my room. "Quickly," he said, as he ushered me in.

I'd spent the afternoon in my room doing what Elizabeth told me. I told her parents that I would be returning to Bulgaria on the earliest flight—her mom purchased the ticket for me while we were on the phone. They were grateful to have their daughter back under their care.

Breaking the news to my mother, however, was even more difficult than I had expected. She didn't believe me. And when she did finally accept it—that her son had disappeared and did not want to be found, which is the story I told, unable to insinuate what Elizabeth and I had agreed to—she screamed at me for failing to locate him. I told her I wouldn't let her talk to me like that, not because I wouldn't, but because it hurt too deeply to hear her in pain.

My flight was set to depart at 6:00 a.m., and I could have easily avoided the patterns man, but he was an expert, as he said so many times. He might know why this happened to us—and how to fix it, should Elizabeth change her mind.

Inside, copies of the front desk Paris map were thumbtacked over every inch of the wall, flaring out and overlapping in corners. He cleared a space for me at the foot of his bed and I sat down. His lips grazed my ear, and he whispered, "The elephant is still in the room. We need to speak in code." Then he took a seat across from me at the desk.

"That's not what I'm here for," I said.

"Remember," he said, before silently mouthing *C-O-D-E*.

"I'm not who you think I am," I said. I straightened my posture.

"We barely know each other. I don't think you're anyone."

"Not that," I said. "I'm referring to something more complicated. It's why I wanted to speak to you."

He flattened his hands over his lap. "Continue," he said.

"I'm not a woman," I said. "I'm a man. My name is Eli Harding. And I'm stuck in this body."

"That's nothing to be ashamed of," he said. He reached over to comfort me. "I used to work with a guy who's a woman."

I flicked his hand away. "I know that."

"You know him?"

"I know it's not anything to be ashamed of."

"It's very brave of you to tell me."

"I'm talking about something different. Something having to do with patterns."

"What kind of patterns?" he asked.

I left nothing out: the dead cat in the street coming to life, the tracksuit man nodding at me, the students I passed en route to Elizabeth's school, Elizabeth waking up as Eli in this very hotel where she studied abroad, my ongoing fear that someone would see through my performance. At the end, I was on the edge of tears, exhausted, bent deeply over my thighs.

"Please help me," I said. "What does it mean?"

The man reached his hand for me again, but this time I didn't bat it away. "Ma'am, I'm so sorry to hear this happened to you. What a horrible and painful story. You don't deserve anything like this, and I can't begin to imagine how painful it is. Divorce is one of the hardest things in the world. I don't know a single person who hasn't had a breakdown after theirs. It tears you open from inside."

I jumped up. "You didn't listen to anything that I told you!"

"I see why you're in so much pain and confused. I want to help you—I do. But what you need now is to rest and relax. You should return to your family. You should be with the people who love you. That's the only way you'll ever begin to heal from what has happened."

"You don't believe me," I said.

"I believe you're going through something traumatic. And I sympathize with you."

"You're the craziest man I've ever met, and *you* don't even believe me."

"I might be a little eccentric, but please do not call me names."

"You're a lunatic!"

"Even flamboyant, or obsessive—I'll cop to obsessive."

I started tearing his maps off the wall, two, three at a time, clawing the paper in bunches. He called hotel security. I fled before they arrived.

# PART V

Elizabeth's parents greeted me in baggage claim, as tall and solemn as sequoias. Her dad had been on the swim team at Harvard, and, more than thirty years later, his shoulders were as broad and muscled as I imagined they'd been in his youth. He kept his head completely shaved, as if trying to remain aerodynamic, and there wasn't a wisp of facial hair on his jaw. Johanna stood a few inches shorter than her husband but was a hair taller than Eli. She was born in Denmark but moved to the States as a baby, and her hair, once an egg-yolky blond, had turned strikingly white with age. Their faces were almost entirely cheekbones. Seeing them—literally looking up at them—explained everything about Elizabeth: She had always looked up to her parents.

"Oh, Lizzy," Johanna said when I got near. She was dressed in a slim brown jacket and gloves, despite being inside. She pulled me in for the type of hug I'd never seen her give to Elizabeth. I was radiating sadness and grateful for the touch. Her father, Henry, rather than wrapping himself around us, waited patiently for Johanna to finish hugging me, then stepped forward to offer an embrace. He kissed me on the temple.

I untangled myself from his arms. Johanna straightened my hair with her palm. She asked how I was feeling and before I could answer, Henry asked if I was hungry. Johanna gave him a chastising look for bringing up something so crass. But I was hungry, and pleased I didn't have to say this myself. I told them food would be good.

Elizabeth rarely stress-ate. She knew better than to be driven by physical need, and I worried that accepting Henry's offer for lunch might expose me. But grief never proceeds how anyone expects. Grief stutters and ruptures and upturns and stomps. When she learned about the death of my father, nearly a decade after he left us, my mother knitted tirelessly through her grief. She was not a knitter. Crafts were never her thing. But she knitted nevertheless, and soon the house was overrun with frustrating sweaters and uneven scarves and one absolutely useless blue belt. My father died in the spring. The clothing was seasonally inappropriate. There was no sense to my mother's decision because it was not a decision. It was an obsession, and inexplicable. During that time, I wouldn't have been surprised to find a life-size replica of my father, entirely twine, eating across from us at the dinner table.

"There's pizza here if you want it," said Elizabeth's dad.

"Henry, she doesn't want pizza," her mom responded, then looked at me. "Unless you want pizza?"

I shook my head.

"See," said her mom.

A wide red light flashed over the baggage carousel. A chute in the center coughed suitcases onto the conveyor belt. People I recognized from the plane gathered their bags, and though I hadn't spoken to them on the flight, seeing them exit the airport saddened me.

Henry asked if I was waiting on a suitcase. I wasn't. We all laughed as if I'd said something funny, desperate for levity.

As we left, Johanna said, "Your father and I have been eating at a place near the hotel—it's not the most exciting food, but . . ." She lowered her voice conspiratorially, the way of Americans who know enough to know better. "You were right."

Over our first three months, on every phone call with her parents, Elizabeth combatted her homesickness by remarking on the cost of everything here, a topic her parents loved to discuss. They were not unwealthy people. Her mother had a private practice, and, from what I gathered, her father was compensated handsomely for his work creating the recipes at Landing, the residency where he worked. They both came from money. They pursued bargains not out of financial necessity but because they wished to maintain the illusion of meritocracy that finding a bargain provided. If they successfully discovered bargains, they were deserving of those bargains, and deserving of the money they saved. This was partly what had led them to the small, liberal town in Michigan where Elizabeth grew up. Her parents swerved away from the lives of their peers, many of whom had settled in expensive, cosmopolitan cities, believing only expensive, cosmopolitan cities could offer the artistic and political values on which meaningful lives were founded.

ISLE McELROY

But they had discovered a refuge where everything that their friends desired could be obtained for a fraction of the cost. Their house was enormous, their mayor a lesbian, the best artists in the world *competed* to visit them. They had so much but needed more, to confirm they had earned everything, and they basked in the cheap Bulgarian prices, as if the country had lowered its cost of living for them. I felt embarrassed for all of us. "It's all very cheap," I said.

"We can go there or anywhere. It's up to you," Johanna said.

"I know a good place," I said. "It's a vegan restaurant. Eli and I used to go there every time we came to Sofia."

"Do you think that's good for you, dear?"

"Johanna, she said she wants to go there, so let's go there." Her dad asked what the restaurant was called and I stumbled through a few incorrect guesses—Sun/Moon, Sunrise/Sunset—before I landed on the right answer: *Day/Night*.

We squeezed into the back seat of a yellow cab idling in front of arrivals. Henry tried to sit in the front, but the driver had a pile of indiscriminate electronics buckled into the passenger seat. I took my rightful place between Elizabeth's parents, with my bag slouched in my lap.

"Your dad's gotten so much better at talking to cab drivers here," said Johanna. "He just hops right into the front seat and starts chatting away, leaves me to fend for myself in the back." They must have shelved a fight to greet me at the airport, and now it expanded like dough rising on the counter.

"I practiced the phrases, so shouldn't I use them?" Henry directed a simple greeting at the cab driver in a surprisingly fluent Bulgarian. He'd studied a few different languages in college, and new ones came easily to him.

The driver cranked up the radio. Johanna laughed childishly at her husband, and when I didn't laugh she took my hand, to comfort me, but nothing about her comfort felt right; it all felt misdirected, or stolen. The driver veered wickedly down slender one-way streets and alleys, narrowly avoiding trash cans, dogs, the occasional child. We sloshed side to side with every turn, Elizabeth's parents taking turns slapping their faces against the back windows. The driver braked in front of the vegan restaurant. He named a price. It was a rip-off, but we deserved it.

Day/Night was built into the tip of a three-story flat-iron building jutting between the legs of a five-pointed intersection. Outside, Bulgarians in parkas and goose down hats braved the weather to eat outside—"Bulgarians always eat outside," Kiril once told me. A waiter greeted us before we reached the entrance and spoke in Bulgarian before registering our confusion. "Where do you want to sit?" he asked.

"Upstairs," I told him.

He delivered us to a tiny square table pressed against a wall beneath a window at the top of the stairs. There were only three chairs. And at the foot of the chairs were toys and games to occupy children. Larger tables were open, tables where our elbows wouldn't plunk against the wall and our knees wouldn't touch, but those tables were reserved.

Elizabeth's parents studied the menu without speaking. They'd carried their fight inside, and now it curled under the table like a dog, liable to bark at any moment.

"Will Eli's mom be coming to see you?" Johanna asked. She made no attempt to hide the superiority in her voice.

"She's flying to Paris today," I said. "She's convinced she might be able to find him, that a mother's grief is more powerful than a wife's."

"What an inconceivable act," she said.

I smiled toothlessly.

"Do you have any idea what he was doing there?" Henry asked.

"That part still doesn't make any sense to me," Johanna said, bitterly. "Why go to Paris, of all places? The most expensive city in the world. Is he planning on living there for the rest of his life?"

Her parents walked a thin bridge between curiosity and anger.

"We don't need to talk about this," I said.

"Do you know how many people I see who refuse to engage with their grief and wind up miles deeper in trauma?"

"How many people?" I asked. Johanna, as an expert, often spoke in grand terms about masses of people suffering from the disorders apparently central to our conversations. After her comments about my own mother visiting, I felt protective of my flawed family and of myself—and I felt obligated to challenge Johanna.

"That's exactly what I'm talking about. You're deflecting. And I want to make sure you take care of yourself. A loss like yours—"

"We don't even know what happened."

"Ambiguous loss is even worse. You lose someone and never get closure. You're in a far more vulnerable spot than you know. I just want you to be healthy."

"Jo," said her dad.

"I know what we said but there's no reason to coddle her now. She knows we care about her, we flew all the way to Bulgaria and honestly I'm frustrated she's treating us like strangers, like we aren't worth talking to about the most devastating thing to ever happen to her."

The waiter interrupted with a greeting in accented English. Henry ordered a beer and Johanna ordered a sparking rosehip tea. I ordered the same beer as Elizabeth's dad.

"You're drinking now?" asked her mom.

"I've always drunk," I said. "Just not around you." I wasn't sure how true this was—had Elizabeth never drunk around her parents? The enormity of her life seemed to expand with every sentence I uttered. There was so little I knew about her, so much I would never uncover, entire years that would remain absent to me. Even the things she had told me about herself—the horse farm neighboring her first childhood home, the queasy joy she felt riding her dad's shoulders as a girl, the Saturday mornings cooking crepes with her mom—were scenes from a movie, remembered but never experienced.

"We're just worried about you," said her mom.

"My husband is gone," I said. *Gone* was the word I'd been using, a word empty enough to mean anything and nothing.

The waiter set down our drinks. He'd heard what I said and made no attempt to take our order. "I will come back," he told us.

"You're not yourself, dear."

"Wouldn't it be even weirder if I were normal? If nothing about the past twelve days changed my outlook on life? If I were politely recommending *cheap* Bulgarian meals?"

"We've traveled so far to see you and you're acting like we've never met. I get that you're grieving but it's not like you to be so disrespectful and distant." She meant no harm by any of this. She merely wanted me to be okay, to believe that I might pass through this unthinkable moment unscathed. Neither she nor Henry, based on the little I knew about them, had ever faced a grief as rigorous as what I was going through now. Her mom handled traumas professionally, yet she couldn't protect her daughter. I felt sorry for her. Perhaps I could have done more to be what she needed. Couldn't I fake it more authentically?

I thanked them both for coming to see me. I did appreciate it, I assured them, they were good parents—great parents—I just wasn't sure how to be human right now.

"Please let us be here for you," Johanna said. This is not what she meant. She wanted me to be there for her by needing her. She wanted to extinguish my grief for her own sense of purpose. She wanted to fix something that couldn't be fixed, which is, perhaps, the intention of every parent—to protect their children from pain.

The waiter returned. In addition to the meals, I ordered lutenitsa, a tomato-based dip served at most meals like bread and butter at Italian places in the States. It was a Bulgarian staple, I assured them. This would give them a taste of the country. When the lutenitsa arrived, they diplomatically dunked their bread in the sauce, hardly gathering any, and praised it with guarded acceptance.

"This is going to take a long time," said her mom. She was sitting to my right, in one of the chairs next to the wall, across from Henry. She appeared to have aged dramatically over the course of the meal, or perhaps the light was hitting her in ways it hadn't before, highlighting the lines reaching out from her eyes. "You're going to need to pace yourself. I've seen too many people try too hard to get better too fast, and one day the pain just swallows them whole. I don't want that to happen to you."

"What would you recommend that I do instead?"

Her dad set down his utensils, first the fork, then the knife overtop like an X. "Feel everything," he said, his voice soft but firm.

"That's what everyone says."

"What your dad means is that this will all be an important time for your growth. You don't want to avoid any emotions that might reappear later in difficult ways."

"When my first wife died," he said, "I tried very hard to push it away."

"She doesn't want to hear about this."

"You were married before?" I asked, but regretted it. Of course Elizabeth would already know.

"Your mom didn't want us to tell you or your brother. And perhaps she was right to keep it from you. It was very short-lived—it wasn't even a marriage. We were engaged when I was in college."

"You don't need to tell me," I said. I'd always found her

parents inscrutable, almost inhumanly so, and though it felt wrong to hear this story before Elizabeth, I desperately wanted to know. Wasn't this the life she chose? I was Elizabeth now—it was my decision whether I listened. "You don't need to tell me," I said, too quietly to truly resist.

"This is a very different set of circumstances," said her mom.

"She was a swimmer as well, maybe the best at the school."

"Harvard wasn't known for its swim program then," Johanna said.

"No need to lie," Henry said.

"She was very talented." Johanna wanted to appear unflappable. She kept her eyes trained on the window to her right. "A perfect athlete and a perfect person. The type of person too good for this world."

"Your mom thinks loving someone before her means that I love her less, as if you can't fit two loves into a life."

"I don't see how this relates. You and Edie were so much younger."

"It's okay," I said. "It's helping to hear about this."

"Your mother thinks I'm still in love with her," said Henry.

"Are you?" I asked.

"It's different when you're younger," he said. "It's much more intense, especially when you lose that person. You never truly know who they are. I know that my feelings, my grief, is grief for a fantasy person, a woman I knew as a child."

"How old was she when she—" I trailed off.

"Twenty," said Elizabeth's mom.

"I can't imagine being engaged at twenty," I said.

"He was desperate to start a life with someone," she said.

Henry straightened up and crossed his arms. Though I knew he was tall, it only occurred to me then how large of a man he was. Large the way a truck or a building is large. He made no attempt to continue his story.

"You and your dad aren't so different," said Johanna. "That's what he tells me. You two are both creatures of feeling, whereas I'm a reasonable person, a person driven by logic. Your dad thinks I put too much weight on endings. I expect too much from conclusions; your dad understands that nothing ever truly comes to an end."

I wanted out of this restaurant just as badly as I didn't want to be anywhere else. "What happened to her?" I asked.

"She died," Johanna said.

"On a mission," added her dad.

"You were religious?"

Elizabeth's mother took on a cute, chipper voice to imitate Henry in love. "Edie was raised Catholic. And she couldn't get it out of her system. She had the biggest heart in the world. She spent every Saturday morning preparing food for homeless shelters. She never missed Mass. Your father didn't *get* any of it. For him it was all so amusing. But also adorable, this thing that would always be hers, these customs that, no matter how hard he tried, he would never be able to access. Religion wasn't cute for Edie. Her life was devoted to a god she couldn't please. And your dad liked that about her—he was never her primary focus. That type of attention disturbed him—it's partly what led him out of photography. A chef can hide; an artist cannot."

I was a decoration inside the room that was her anger.

"I forgot to mention how pretty she was. Edie. Also a genius."

"She wasn't that pretty," he said.

"Which of course made her even more charming. So close to perfect. Just a little bit off. She had space to expand into someone better than she already was."

I had never seen Johanna this way. And, based on how Elizabeth spoke about her, as a stable and nurturing force in her life, I doubted she'd ever seen her this way either. This was likely the most emotion she had ever shown in front of her daughter. She seemed ready to pull a rumpled pack of cigarettes from her purse and light up in the restaurant, but instead she tucked a loose strand of hair to where it belonged behind her left ear and leaned back in her chair, as if anticipating a show.

"You're making Lizzy uncomfortable," said her dad.

"We're all uncomfortable, Henry. But remember: We're supposed to be feeling our feelings. Isn't that what you told her? We're getting it out of our systems—and I bet Elizabeth appreciates the distraction. Why fret about her negligent husband?"

"Is that what you think of him?" I asked. "That Eli was negligent?"

"His heart was in the right place," she said. "He meant well. That is for certain. But he was never on the same level as you. I know that you loved him—you've always been so good at loving people beneath you. It's one of your charms. You love people who aren't worth your time. I never knew how to do it myself."

"Eli wasn't beneath me."

"What your mom means is that we worked hard to give you the life you're living. And you worked very hard to run with every opportunity that came your way. Some parents don't work as hard as we worked."

"I don't see why we're dancing around it," Johanna said. "We've all met his mother. We all know what she's like. I have no doubt she did her best with that boy, but sometimes your best just isn't enough."

"That's a very cruel thing to say," I said.

"We aren't cruel people," Johanna said. "We're honest people. We're people with standards and taste. There's a difference. You're the same way. Of course you toss those standards aside when you love someone—remember Benny, the boy you dated at Hinneman?"

"Benny was nice," I said. I knew nothing about Benny but would now defend every boy Elizabeth had dated to my death.

"You're a critical person because we were critical people. And Eli is how he is because of his mother and father."

"Eli worked very hard to make a different life for himself." This was never something that I had explicitly thought about myself but a compliment Elizabeth paid me after leaving my mother's house one year after Christmas. *I'm so proud of you for escaping that house*, she had said. Her sentiment stunned me. It had never occurred to me that I had been living a difficult life—to me, it was merely a life, and what I felt after her comment wasn't pride but shame, a feeling given a second life after years existing dormant inside me.

"Everything settles back to where it began. From what I gathered his parents—especially his father—were flighty and unpredictable people. And look what happens: He abandoned you without warning. What type of person would do such a thing? I don't get it. I hope to never get it—it's awful. I'm not saying it isn't okay to fall out of love with your partner. Those things *happen*. Nothing can prevent that. I've seen it happen to people who'd never expect it, people who spend thirty years driven by bottomless love who wake up one morning to find the well is as dry as a ditch. But when that happens they act like adults. They plan. Arrangements are made. But this. I don't like it. And it's exactly what I could've told you would happen."

"She doesn't like seeing someone hurt you so badly," said Henry. "And he hurt all of us. To us, Eli was family."

"He might be a sociopath for all that I know. Those people never think of anyone else but themselves. I've seen a few in my practice. But you never know until they suddenly snap. They harbor all this ill will. They hide it like magicians. And then out of nowhere—kaboom!—they contrive some event that will cause you the greatest and most personal pain."

"You don't know anything," I said.

"We know far more than you think," she said.

"Let's not talk about this here, okay?" said Henry.

"You're absolutely right," said Johanna. "We're supposed to be talking about Edie and your one timeless love. The perfect angel who left this world too early."

I was relieved to be in a country where so few people spoke English. Her parents argued with practiced control. For all anyone knew, they were discussing insurance plans or deciding where to go shopping after the meal. Anger had never been so deftly contained. It frightened me even more than the shouting I'd witnessed between my mother and her husbands.

"You act like I'm the only one to ever love anyone else," Henry said. He took an obnoxious swig from his beer. They were entirely different people from the ones I had known. Perhaps the grief they assumed for Elizabeth was contagious, toppling the lives they'd worked so hard to protect. The last twelve days had pried the lid off every regret they kept bottled up; spilling onto the table were dozens of parallel lives. "Did you know your mom had an affair?"

"Don't exaggerate."

"But she could have had an affair, which she has made very clear to me. She wants me to know something could have happened."

"Henry, weren't you just saying that these aren't conversations to have with our daughter?"

"So now you're concerned about Elizabeth's innocence?"

Any other time, I would have listened to the dull ache of discomfort in my stomach, this feeling of secondhand shame, and asked them to change the subject. But I wanted away from my feelings. My grief was cumulative. Existential. I had been dumped both by Elizabeth and by myself. I'd lost my wife. A tragedy. And I had lost my own life and my body. An uncanny tragedy. Over the past twenty-four hours, as my feet ached from walking in slippers, my muscles exhausted in ways they rarely were—because I ignored my own pain—I felt an intense longing for the body I knew. My own wouldn't have been so sore. My body was ox-like, calloused from years of overexertion and repressed trauma. Gone were the ankles that cracked when I rotated them in circles, the patches of hair frothing at the top of my chest, the mangled scar on my thumb where broken glass had entered the skin, the tender clench of my stomach after I ate something too spicy and rich. I missed my dick. I missed the single fold of fat on my abdomen. I missed my belly button—Elizabeth had an outie. I missed my biceps, which were not large but sculpted. I missed picking my ears. More things, surely, things I hadn't even realized I missed yet. They could say whatever they wanted, no matter how uncomfortable it made me, so long as it meant leaving my mind for a few minutes. I asked Elizabeth's dad to say more about the affair.

"It was shortly after your brother was born," he said. He leaned conspiratorially close. "And don't tell your brother any of this. He's the sensitive one. He's not as secure as you are."

Channeling Elizabeth, I said, "You're always babying him."

"Because he's the baby," said Johanna. That was the end of that.

The waiter cleared our plates and Henry ordered a second beer and a second for me. I expected Johanna to get in on the action, but she ordered another sparkling tea.

"He was a friend of mine. A sculptor—the jocks of the art world."

"A practicing artist," Johanna said, to hurt her husband.

The waiter dropped off the drinks. "He and I knew each other from RISD. Casey. We were competitive but friendly. I was the far more talented one but art is never about talent. It's about effort. Casey kept at it. I took jobs photographing food, which evolved into preparing food—I wanted something more active—and your mom and I moved to Michigan to start a family, which we had always wanted to do.

"Casey moved to Manhattan, to be in the scene. Don't take what I'm saying the wrong way. Casey had something. He had a vision. He lacked just about every other discernible skill—including the patience to heighten his technical skills. But if you have vision, you can go very far in the art world, so long as you find a way to keep working."

"Was he rich?" I asked.

"Not only that. He was handsome. He had those boyish looks that some artists inhabit so easily; he always looked a little surprised. It's how men look when they never grow up. Common to artists who spend their lives inside their imaginations. There was something untouched about Casey. That's what people found handsome about him. It's what attracted your mom. Because your mom and I, as parents we were decidedly touched.

"Casey arrived at Landing eight weeks after your brother was born. Your mom was on maternity leave and I was working nonstop. She understood I wasn't avoiding the family. But she was also lonely. She'd spent so much time alone and was tired of herself, tired of her body and of her children."

"That's not how I put it," she said.

"That is how you put it," he said.

She flicked her wrist, a wave of acceptance.

"Some women love to be pregnant. That's how your mom put it. Some women love seeing their bodies transform—but she didn't. It's a miracle, sure, but to her it was also grotesque. I never made her feel that way. I was a very supportive husband."

"No one is saying you weren't," she said.

"You were a small baby. But your brother—what was the word you used?"

"Remodeled."

"She was convinced I no longer found her attractive."

"This would be a good time to say that you still find me attractive."

"Honey, I still find you attractive," he said, in the tone of a man verifying his address over the phone.

"Your father is such a romantic."

"I'm susceptible to exhaustion, just like anyone else. I pass through romantic lapses. And this lapse came at a terrible time because your mom, she needed things," he said. "And during my lapse in affection, Casey arrives in small-town Michigan from his studio in Manhattan. He was a man I could have been if I'd never committed to you and your mom and your brother. He was charming. The way a knife can be charming. I was jealous of him for living this alternate life, but I also felt superior to him, because I had, after all, settled down. I gave up the hustle. And I wanted to show him how wonderful life could be with a family.

"I helped him unpack the day he arrived and suggested he come over the following evening at seven o'clock, only half an hour after I got off work. It was selfish to invite him to a dinner that I wouldn't prepare in a house that I wouldn't clean. Your mom hadn't seen him in four years; she only knew him through the conduit of my envy. She resented me for this. She had every right to chew me out. But she's not that type of person. She aims to please—it's one of the best things about her."

"Your dad didn't mean to neglect me," said Johanna. "People rarely intend to cause harm. The ones who cause premeditated harm—those ones are dangerous. They're the ones who trouble me. But that wasn't your father. He was busy—the simplest explanation is most often correct. He couldn't give me what I needed."

"The thing about affairs, according to your mom, is that they're all the same in such devastating and predictable ways. Affairs are flickers of hope. Escape hatches."

"I've seen many people through their affairs," she added.

"It's easy to confuse wanting to be someone with wanting to be with them."

"He was a professional artist," she said with a shrug. "I once wanted to be an artist."

"Casey was supposed to come over at seven, but he finished his work earlier than he expected. He'd walked to the house—four miles. It's the kind of walk a person can make when their days stretch before them like fields. You and your brother occupied every quiet minute of your mom's life.

"Casey arrived with a bottle of champagne to celebrate our reunion, and when he saw the state of the house, heard your brother wailing and spied you sitting cross-armed at the table, in time-out for knocking photos off the wall, he asked how he could help. She told him he couldn't help with something she hadn't even begun to prepare. 'Watch me,' he said, and tossed an apron over his neck. He poured your mom a glass of champagne, her first drink since your brother was born, and told her to go relax.

"An hour later, I arrived home to the scent of deglazing lamb and your mother sitting on the counter with you in her lap, watching Casey finish the meal. It was a politely tense evening. Every detail of his life poked me like a fork under the table. I was obsessed with him, so threatened and envious, and I didn't even notice your mom falling in love."

"It was a crush," she said.

"At the end of the night, your mom knew she needed to see him again. Alone, that is. The following week, she dropped you and your brother off with a friend who owed her a favor and drove to Landing to see Casey. Your mom didn't tell me she was coming. She felt terrible for wanting someone so badly merely because he'd given her an hour of rest. Because he was *charming*, as if charm isn't everywhere. He couldn't give her what I could—commitment, stability, love—and that's what drew her to Casey. She could imagine destroying her life in exchange for a quick spell of lust.

"Perhaps you've never experienced this need to be with someone else, or to be someone else. You haven't even been married six months. Your mom and I had been married for six years. She assures me she wasn't falling out of love with me, but she was restless. She longed for romance, passion, and time."

"Your dad wasn't incapable of those things," Johanna said. "But he didn't have room for me in his life—not anymore." She tapped my wrist. "This isn't a sexual story, dear. I promise you. You don't have to look so disgusted."

It hadn't occurred to me that I might appear disgusted—but I kept my face as it was. Elizabeth would surely feel the same way learning about her parents' affairs.

"It's a story of wanting," Johanna said. "Of imagination curtailed."

"Your mom didn't warn Casey that she was coming. She liked the idea of surprising him—the ultimate act of passion. When she arrived at Landing, she checked in with Maud at the office to see where Casey was staying. Maud asked whether she had a message for me. 'He's off picking up supplies,' she added. Your mom told her she needed to drop something off for an artist. 'Casey Fitzpatrick,' she said. 'He visited for dinner a few nights ago and forgot something at our place.' Maud offered to hold it for him at the office, and your mom, with no item to give, told Maud the item was personal, that he would prefer to receive it directly."

"Don't make me sound so manipulative," Johanna said.

"No one said you were manipulative, but you lied."

"A white lie."

"I'm not arguing that."

"I'm certain Maud saw right through me," Johanna said. "Nothing she said, just a feeling. 'These artists are so particular,' she told me. 'He probably needs it to work.' I told her I was sure that he did. It was an act of kindness. She helped me construct an alibi."

"She told your mom where he was staying."

"Dunleavy," she said. Her response was clipped; she had grown tired of Henry speaking for her. He leaned back in his chair. "I was scared I'd cross paths with your dad, but this made everything more illicit and fun. This was unlike anything I'd ever done. And I loved becoming this other person—I wasn't sure how long it would last.

"Dunleavy was a hunched yellow cabin at the tip of a gravel driveway twenty minutes from the office by foot. A rusty gray bike tilted against the front porch. It was your father's old bike—he'd donated it to Landing when he bought a new one. Everything was too real, then. I turned around, ready to run home, but Casey's door slapped open and he called my name, like I was a cat he wished to summon inside. I put on a face of surprise, as if I were as shocked to see Casey as he was to see me. He made a big sweeping wave and invited me in. It was the reason I'd come here, after all, and despite the stone in my stomach, I walked to the—"

A metallic crash in the street stilled every conversation. The other diners crowded around us to peer out the window next to our table. I scrunched alongside them, my face at the glass. A yellow cab had rammed into the front of a silver BMW. The Bulgarians around us asked what had happened, and Henry repeated, "English." The Bulgarians filed outside to join the ceremony of onlookers. Henry and Johanna angled their faces toward the window and leaned closer to it. I stood, to get a clear look at the street, and when I lowered my eyes, to the ledge just under the window, Johanna slid her hand into the welcome palm of her husband.

I resigned the fellowship position. Elizabeth's parents drove me back to help pack the apartment into suitcases. They insisted this would provide closure—as much as was possible.

"This is what you need," Johanna said repeatedly on the drive. She was convincing herself more than me.

There were no open spots in front of the apartment building when we arrived. Henry let us out and sped off to park. The temperature had dropped dramatically since I'd left, and, in the shadow of the building, I shivered so forcefully that Johanna put her arm around me.

"Elizabeth!" I heard. Kiril was walking toward us from the café.

"That's Kiril," I said, assuming that Elizabeth must have told her about Kiril and Desi. But her face didn't register the name, and I quickly, quietly, explained who they were.

"You're back from your vacation!" he said. He was dressed in pale jeans and a loose navy blue sweater, a flour-spotted apron tied around his waist. He'd shaved his beard while I was gone, and, in the cold, his face was shrimpishly pink.

"That's very disrespectful," Johanna said.

"He doesn't know," I said.

"What don't I know?" he asked. In only a few months, I had gathered that Kiril hated being walled off from gossip. Living in America shaped his relationship to secrets. He had a justified paranoia, the outsider's fear that others might be talking about him.

"It's a long story," I said, knowing that he would invite us inside.

"Are you okay?" he asked. He put his hand on my arm—likely the first time he'd ever touched Elizabeth so tenderly. "Come have a cup of coffee."

"Thank you, but we have so much to take care of today," Johanna said.

"We'd love that," I said. "Kiril, this is Johanna. My mother." It was the first time I'd referred to her as my mother to anyone else.

"We really must be going," Johanna said.

I followed Kiril into the café. I wasn't prepared to reenter that apartment with Elizabeth's parents and was relieved to push that reckoning further into the future.

Inside, Desi was talking to a middle-aged woman in Bulgarian. She waved at us without breaking the conversation. Kiril sat Johanna and me down on the scratchy yellow couch beneath the TV. The news stations reported on the massacre in

Paris, splicing in footage from the Turkish border. I didn't need to read Bulgarian to know who they were blaming.

"I should find Dad," Johanna said. That instant, he passed the window beside us, and I knocked on the glass to catch his attention. He was bewildered, as if we were fish in a tank.

Kiril returned with two red cups of espresso. Henry entered, and Kiril greeted him in Bulgarian. Henry pointed at us and said, "I'm with them."

"He's Elizabeth's dad," Johanna said.

"Coffee?" Kiril asked.

"He'll drink mine," Johanna answered.

Henry squeezed in beside us on the couch. Desi wouldn't look over at me, even after the customer left. Perhaps she was ashamed to see me after what I had witnessed between her and Kiril.

Kiril slid a chair from one of the small round tables to the couch. We looked like family therapy clients, Kiril our therapist. "When is Eli coming back?" he asked.

"He's not coming back," said Johanna.

"What does that mean?" he asked.

We said nothing. Kiril brought his hands to his face as if he might cry. I felt sick over his grief, wishing that I could explain it away.

"Do you think that he might have . . . you know?"

The insinuation was suicide, and I felt exposed—or rather the awareness that I had never hidden myself from anyone, not even strangers. I was so obvious to everyone, including a man I'd known only for months. Johanna waited for me to answer, and I eventually said, "All we know is he's missing."

"So he might not really be gone?" he asked.

"This is a family matter," said Henry.

After learning what they thought about me at the vegan restaurant, I no longer wished to stow away in their family. They believed in family as an impermeable lockbox that nothing should enter or escape. I hated that notion of family. It valorized the accident of bloodline over all else. Kiril and Desi often frustrated me; they frustrated Elizabeth even more; but they had also looked after us: They helped us rent cars and navigate paying utilities and served us espresso and cookies and chatted on the afternoons we were so unapproachably lonely. Why shouldn't they know what we knew? "I know you were close," I said to Kiril. "But the truth is we just don't know what happened yet. And we're all very confused."

"Did he have friends in the city?" Kiril asked. "Perhaps he is staying with them?"

"Eli doesn't have friends anywhere," I said.

He flinched, startled by the cruelty of my comment.

"I mean I don't know—I don't know who he knows. It's all still so confusing."

"People don't normally disappear like this," Johanna said. "Not anymore."

Kiril spun to check on Desi. She handed cash to a customer.

Henry sipped espresso through his teeth. The drink seemed to make him physically ill.

The customer left and Kiril waved Desi over. She approached smiling, introduced herself to Elizabeth's parents. But our faces betrayed the subject of our conversation. Kiril caught her up in Bulgarian. Desi looked at me after he finished, desperate to be told what she'd heard wasn't true. "I'm so sorry," she said. She crouched and clasped my hands, casting Elizabeth's parents aside. They angled away from me. "I'm so, *so* sorry," she repeated.

Kiril pulled over another chair and Desi joined our quartet of grief.

"We don't know all the details," said Johanna, like a doll capable of only one phrase.

"We should really be going," said Henry.

"How can you know that he's not coming back?" Desi was hunched forward into the center of our circle, increasingly disturbed by what she had learned.

"All we know is he doesn't want to be here. We have to accept it," said Johanna.

"It's very painful," said Henry. "You never prepare for these things."

"He will come back," Desi said. "You didn't find him because he's probably already on his way back to you." If she had returned to *her* husband after their fight at the fish house, then surely my husband would return to me. He needed time to clear his thoughts. The same thing she needed. It was natural for someone to explode and leave—as it was natural for them to return. The messy desire she'd felt in the restaurant was a temporary condition. She wanted everything to be how it was—but Eli's disappearance was proof that some lives and relationships could not be reestablished. They are better left broken.

Desi was living inside something broken, and I got the sense that she envied me for my grief and confusion. Better this loss than hers: the loss of the desire she had felt for the chef from the hotel, desire that briefly rose within her again before getting snuffed out when she returned to her husband. She wanted me alongside her, confronting the great yawn of commitment. But she would have to face this alone.

A man entered the café. I had seen him dozens of times in the city—a background character in my life, just as I was a background character in his. Kiril stood, but Desi rushed to the register first and greeted the man with a chipper Bulgarian welcome. We sat like a paused movie, waiting for Desi to return. After the man left, she dusted her hands and slipped into the kitchen.

"She doesn't handle stress very well," Kiril said. "I haven't told you, but we are making a lot of changes around here. For the better. That is why I was so happy today—I'm sorry but it really was a special day. When I saw you, I wanted to tell you the news." He still wanted to tell us the news. A smile roamed behind his mouth like a cat under a blanket.

"We should be leaving," Johanna said.

"Thank you so much," said Henry. He set the espresso cup on Desi's empty chair.

"We could all use some good news," I said. I expected him to tell us that he and Desi were pregnant—or that they had finally decided to try.

He angled forward, wrists on his knees, and spoke with conspiratorial glee: "We're going to buy a pizza oven." When we said nothing, he added: "For the store!"

"But you're a coffee shop," I said.

"Not anymore," Kiril said.

The Landing artist residency had recently installed a pizza oven in its kitchen. It had been Henry's idea—a way to create community among the artists; once a month, they would join the staff for a huge pizza party. He was proud of the initiative, and according to surveys, it had successfully heightened morale at the residency. He asked Kiril how much the oven would cost.

Kiril named the cost of the pizza oven. "Can you believe it's so cheap?" he said.

"That sounds very high-quality," Henry said, stunned by the figure.

"We were very lucky," Kiril said. "The men came in here by accident, looking to buy a birthday cake to bring back to Plovdiv, and as we talked he told me he sells oven supplies."

Desi wasn't pregnant—but Kiril was, with a future that hardly included her. The money they'd been saving to move out of his parents' house, the foundation for having a child, would be spent on this oven.

"There are already so many pizza places in town," I said.

"No place as good as ours will be," he said. "We'll heat them in under five minutes."

"You might burn the crusts at that heat," Henry said.

"The man assured me it cooks at a perfect temperature."

Desi exited the kitchen carrying a massive sheet pan bubbled with rosemary scones—their most popular flavor. She and Kiril traded comments in Bulgarian, and Desi shook her head, proceeded to stock the display.

"We are both very excited," he said.

"I'm not feeling well," I said.

"Of course," Kiril said. "I got too carried away. I wanted to lighten the mood."

I thanked him. Then I congratulated him. Then I made an excuse about having traveled so much over the past week. I was jet-lagged, depressed.

"Thank you for inviting us in," Johanna said.

"You're saying this man came in off the street looking for a cake?" Henry asked. He didn't buy it, and he appeared ready to break to Kiril that he had been scammed.

"Elizabeth's not feeling well," Johanna said.

"You can't get any luckier," Kiril said to Henry. His excitement had devolved into a kind of fragile poise. Kiril knew that the man hadn't stumbled in by accident. He wasn't a small-town bumpkin incapable of seeing through an obvious scam. He was a man who needed to believe in something, and he had chosen to believe in making a killing off artisanal pizzas in a town where people could barely afford his pastries. Henry was the gullible one for believing that only he could see the oven man for the charlatan he was. Henry's sense of exceptionalism was the greatest delusion in the room; Kiril, at least, had chosen delusion.

Kiril and Desi expressed their deepest condolences as we

left. As she hugged me, she leaned close to my ear, and I tensed, expecting her to whisper something to me, some utterance of understanding meant only for me, some wisdom I could carry decades into the future. She said nothing. She released me. She told Elizabeth's parents how lovely it was to meet them.

My mother flew into Paris the same day I left, desperate for any detail suggesting her son would return. She knew what I meant by "gone" and refused to believe it, not without a body confirming her fears. I ached to relieve her grief. But I had promised Elizabeth to hold on to this secret—this awful, absurd secret that set the foundation for our new lives—and couldn't betray her, not even to protect my own mother from pain. In Paris, she sent an email telling me she would fly to Bulgaria to retrieve Eli's possessions. She asked me to prepare his items for her. Eli was no longer Elizabeth's responsibility, my mother's urgency seemed to imply. Our marriage was a temporary condition. Death had made him hers again.

This is, at least, how Johanna described it as we boxed up Eli's stuff. "If this happened to you," she said, "I wouldn't want Eli involved. Parents say they can never imagine burying their child, but it is the only thing we imagine. The movie plays nonstop in the backs of our brains. From the instant we know you exist we fear learning you don't. Beneath everything we do is a plan: how we would act if we lost you."

"What would you do?" I asked.

"That's not something I care to answer right now," she said.

Henry dragged tape over the flaps of a full box of books, purposefully interrupting.

"I'm too superstitious to risk bringing these plans into the world."

"Finished another box," Henry said, like we hadn't heard the tape.

"How quickly do you think you would know?" I asked.

"Know what?"

"Know that something happened to me."

Henry filled a glass of water at the faucet then emptied it in one gulp; he needed to occupy his hands at every moment.

"We would know the instant it happened," Johanna said. "Is that what you want to hear?"

"What if I didn't die." I don't know what I wanted. Perhaps I wished for some proof that, for all of her flaws, my mother's love for me was superior to theirs for their daughter.

"This isn't a healthy conversation," Johanna said. "It concerns me that you're having these thoughts. Are you thinking of harming yourself?"

"I'm not having *these* thoughts. I'm asking you a question."

"Are you *asking* whether we'd know if something bad happened to you? That's a horrible accusation to make against your parents. It's about the worst thing you could say."

"No one wants another argument today," Henry said. He was ballooning with water by now, emptying glass after glass, refill after refill, like a machine built to avoid.

I told them I was stressed, and angry, and I wasn't sure how to act. I apologized.

Johanna assured me I wasn't the only angry one here. "What happened to you is a tragedy," she said. "You won't even be able to finish your fellowship. He took this from you. He took your future. All to do what—gallivant around Paris?"

"I could finish my term if I wanted to."

"But no one expects you to."

"It's kind of them to excuse you," Henry said. "Accept the kindness."

"I guess I'm hardly an ambassador for American interests in my condition," I said.

Elizabeth's parents laughed. I hadn't realized I was telling a joke, but I laughed too. No one had ever said it so baldly before: I was here to advance American interests.

"They've already selected a teacher from Sofia to replace me."

"What do you want to keep of Eli's stuff?" Johanna asked.

"His mother asked me to keep everything for her to look through when she arrives."

"You two were married. If there's something important to you, you deserve it."

Their superficial propriety infuriated me. They worked so hard to appear like good people, lobbing judgments onto strangers they assumed were beneath them, people like my mother, whose requests they ignored out of convenience, and for the first time I saw them for who they were in all their pain and anger and smallness and love. Of course they prioritized their daughter over my mother. They were correct in the allegiance they formed, and I despised them for it. I asked them to leave.

"We're planning on getting dinner soon. You're welcome to join us. It might help you to leave the apartment for a little while."

"I need the night to myself."

"We were thinking we'd stay here," Johanna said.

"There are plenty of hotels in the city. Even last minute, it won't cost you too much."

"You're sure you don't want to come with us for dinner? I'm worried you won't eat in your condition."

"What condition is that?"

"Why are you making this so difficult? You're depressed. Grieving. You isolate when you're not feeling well and I don't want you to suffer any more than you need to."

"She wants us to leave," Henry said.

"It's always about her," Johanna said. "Every single time it's about her." This argument was decades in the making, and she spoke with more exhaustion than anger. She was tired of returning to a conflict that would never resolve.

"I'm the one who lost my husband," I said. I hated becoming the person Elizabeth believed me to be—a person who weaponized my pain—but she was right about me. She was always right. This is how I protected myself.

"This won't last forever," Johanna said. "You're in pain now but you won't be in pain in the future and you need to start acting like you *have* a future, because you do."

"Not even two weeks have passed."

Johanna sat on the arm of the couch, ashamed of what she had said. It wasn't right for her to treat me with such chilliness after so little time had elapsed. When she finally spoke, she said, "Gratitude. That's the difference between you and your brother. He is grateful for the opportunities we provided for him. You wanted more. You want more from every single person around you—your dad and I put our lives on pause to fly here to be with you. Do you think that's easy? Do you think Landing is happy? Do you know what it's like to tell clients I can't see them this week—clients who *need* me? And you're treating us like neighbors who popped in uninvited. We love you, Elizabeth. But you take so much for granted. You assume we're going to be there for you—and when we can, we will be. But we are not obligated to do this. We're doing it because we love you. Look at Eli's mother. We never would have waited so long to come looking for you. The instant you were in trouble, we came to see you. We're here to support you and if you don't want our support, we won't give it to you. But think hard before you treat us like shit."

I'd never heard her curse before, and the word came out blocky and quiet, but not without its intended effect: I felt ashamed of myself.

"I think we could all benefit from some time apart," Henry said. He returned his water cup to the cabinet. "It's been such a difficult week."

In these situations, a mature person would say, "I don't want to say something I'll later regret" and say nothing. That same person would distance herself from a tense situation and return once her anger had cooled. Elizabeth was one of these people. I wasn't. I always said the things I later regretted, and, when an opportunity presented itself to act differently, to be better, I rarely took it. Luckily, before I could say what I knew I would regret, that she ought to stay the fuck out of my life if she considered me so ungrateful, before I could uncork years of Elizabeth's exasperated complaints about her parents, her phone started ringing.

My mom's full name appeared on the screen. What better proof did we need that she would know when I was in trouble?

Johanna asked if I planned on answering.

"We're in the middle of something," I said. The phone stopped ringing and started ringing again. Johanna gave me an *answer it* look. I swiped the green circle to the right. "Hel—"

"I found him!" she said. "On the street! He was eating outside at a café and I—I nearly killed him myself I was so angry."

"The body?"

"Hold on—I'll give it." There was a windy, scraping sound as the phone shuffled hands.

"It's me," Elizabeth said.

"They found you," I said.

"They found me," she said.

Elizabeth grew up at the end of a long gravel driveway tilted down like a ladle, in an A-frame house the color of denim left unloved in the sun, its deck looping around like a belt. She knew the house the way cats know their own fur. She knew how sunlight breathed into the living room on summer afternoons, igniting the armchairs under the windows. She knew where the spices were kept and how the blankets were folded before being tucked in the ottoman. She knew how to turn the kitchen faucet handles so as not to burn yourself while washing dishes—though hot enough to ensure a thorough cleaning. She knew where the family dog—the one who bit her when she was girl—was buried and the difference in the cadence between her dad descending the steps and her mom and how to prepare herself for a conversation depending on who was approaching. She knew when to look for hummingbirds gracing the garden. Some books in the living room were mere decoration, whereas others' pages were thumb-softened from countless rereadings, and Elizabeth knew to only reference the reread books in conversation, their passages knitted into the family story like myths. The good towels—the ones for the guests—were kept on the bottom shelf of the cabinet next to the bathroom. Flashlights could be found in the pantry. The house was not made for the winter and not for the summer, its walls permeable but unbreezy; the only perfect place in the house was the deck during the last few weeks of spring, before summer decided to really show off. She loved to lounge on the deck with her parents, eating dinner around a small circular table beneath an umbrella, everyone reading magazines or newspapers and volleying new, riveting facts between bites of the meal. This was the machinery that made her family a family.

But now she couldn't be herself in this place—no, she had to pretend to be a stranger, to know nothing about it, to love nothing about it, or to love it as a tourist would love it, without intimacy and memory and possession and feeling. She and Eli returned to her parents' home out of convenience. They agreed they ought to stay together after all they had experienced; this house was better suited to carry them forward. Eli did not disagree. He was ashamed of having caused his mother immeasurable grief, all of which he could have prevented, and he couldn't stand the idea of seeing her every day.

The couple sat across from each other on her childhood bed, the covers tucked hotelishly taut under the mattress. She tried to sit cross-legged the way she liked, but Eli's body wouldn't cooperate. She advised him how to sit how she liked, the left leg winged behind the right. "This is where you find the good towels," she said. "This is what you say when you answer the phone. This is how much dinner you eat. This is how—are you listening?"

Eli repeated every word she had said back to her.

"This is how you shake your head when my mom brings up the Hendersons. This is what you say when my dad talks about Benjamin Grave, the director of Landing, his boss. When my aunt Cindy is mentioned—and always *awe-nt*, never *ant*—don't say anything, you've learned to not have opinions about her. Giggle when anyone talks about Grandmother Ana. She is not a serious person."

Hours later, as Eli slept, it occurred to Elizabeth that she might have to explain herself to him for the rest of her life, that there was no way to teach someone how to be someone else, that eventually his Elizabeth would become the true Elizabeth, no matter how hard she worked to maintain her history inside the body that used to be hers, that people would think, *Elizabeth changed*, and they would accept her, or tolerate her, as if whatever inconsistencies they recognized were simply the inconsistencies that accrue over the course of a life, changes in habit and taste and desire, and she, the true Elizabeth, would be swallowed whole like a stone in a stomach.

It was already happening. Eli slept peacefully on his side, unbothered by her tossing, hugging a pillow to his chest the way he had always slept, and Elizabeth felt as if she were watching a recording of herself imitating her husband. She had never slept with such equanimity. She slept okay before they started dating—though she couldn't claim to be a good sleeper—used to watch him sleep, in Arizona, wondering whether he'd taken this from her, her sleep, as if a relationship only came with a set number of hours and he'd claimed them all for himself. He fell into beds the way anchors fell into oceans, no matter the bed, while Elizabeth stayed awake worrying over endings for stories and things she had said she wished to unsay.

She shook him awake. It was mean to wake him, but every marriage allowed for the occasional cruelty, like an unsuitable outfit tried on at the store before being placed back on the rack. "There's more I need to tell you."

Eli yawned.

"And no it can't wait until morning."

Because she was not the marrying type or the man-fixing type or the type to play bar trivia or the type to obsess over the TV show everyone's watching or the type to love someone who couldn't spot the difference between Frankenthaler and Nevelson or the type to put her life ahead of her art, the type to return home, saddened and baffled, to a house she loved but never wanted to live in again, never like this, as a child starting over again, then Eli needed to not be the type, never the type, and he couldn't sleep until he wasn't.

"There are things you won't be able to plan for," he said. "You can plan for the towels and the flashlights and the recycling and the aunts, but at some point you'll have to trust me, because all I can do is aspire to the version of you I find the most accurate, which is the version of you that I love, the kind and brilliant and generous person—a person who would, I truly believe, let her partner sleep through the night."

She fell into the day of their wedding, bending back to the earth in his arms, to how he made her feel small the way only a parent makes you feel small, small like a torn flower in the shallow scoop of a palm. Was it this that she wanted? It couldn't be.

"Are we gonna get through this?" she asked.

"I think so," he said.

"Will we be okay is what I'm asking."

"Of course we'll be okay."

"What makes you so sure about that?"

"Nothing," he said.

PART VI

**A** miracle.

That is how Elizabeth described Eli's return. I, however, consider it shameful after all I had said to Elizabeth about her husband. I never should have opened my mouth, but what right did I have keeping my thoughts to myself? What Eli did to my daughter was cruel and unhinged. What type of person—there's no use in asking these questions. I know better than to ask what cannot be answered—or worse, what has an obvious answer.

"Good morning," I now say to the man who abandoned my daughter.

"How are you?" I ask the man who tried to ruin her life.

"Dinner is ready," I tell the sociopath on my couch.

My punishment is to pretend I care about this person for the sake of my daughter. This is the curse of motherhood. You have no control over your child's mistakes. You watch those mistakes unfold in silence. This silence is called love. A mother's advice will never be heeded. Every mother is Cassandra fruitlessly unloading the future on an unlistening family. I didn't listen to my mother and she didn't listen to hers and she to hers and she to hers. I would have lost all respect for Elizabeth if she listened to me.

But she wanted to work on things. Safely. Far from the trauma of their apartment in Europe. So they moved back to Michigan to live with Henry and me, into the house where Elizabeth was raised. We became a family. And no one cared what I thought. No one cared what Eli did to our daughter. I've known men like him, and it doesn't do any good to tell the women who love them who they are. Elizabeth's husband was back. Why should it matter what type of person he is?

THREE WEEKS AFTER THEY RETURNED HOME, WE FOUND ourselves gathered together for a special occasion: Ceremony Day at Landing. On this day, Landing invites an artist of major renown to deliver a lecture about The State of the Arts inside an auditorium on campus. The lectures are meant to inspire and warn. Tickets cost two hundred dollars. Henry receives six free tickets in exchange for his ongoing acceptance of two paltry weeks of vacation.

This year's speaker was Ellen Locke, a Scottish writer renowned for her autobiographical portraits of motherhood and late middle age. She is the type of writer I might have become had I continued pursuing a writing career—had I followed my college ambitions. She possesses an almost unbearable sense of freedom and conviction. I admire her so that I might defend against the oblivion of my envy. My life is full of people like this. Those I cannot help but support and appreciate lest I succumb to bitterness. I have read none of Locke's books, though I have nearly memorized every interview she's ever given. I am terrified of the actual books because in them I might find that version of myself that I will never become.

Henry and I go to Ceremony Day every year. It falls on the Monday before Christmas. Normally Elizabeth and Liam are home to join us. This year, though, Liam is in Seattle with his girlfriend and her family—his first Christmas away from home. Liam assured me he would return home for New Year's, but I doubt he will. He and Elizabeth have been distant since she returned. To him, she seems different. He and his girlfriend have been dating for only a few months, and as serious as they are, it is too soon to spend a holiday with her parents. I didn't try to convince Liam to come home. He was right. Elizabeth *was* different, and, had she been my sister, I would have avoided her too.

Elizabeth now moves through the house with a kind of caution I find unnerving. She has forgotten obvious details—where we keep extra towels, what day we take out the trash. She recently asked me to remind her of our zip code. It hasn't been *that* long since she lived here. I did my best to not make her feel bad for forgetting these things. She has been through so much. And I admire her resilience. Here she is. Alive. Well. Making the most of her life.

For Christmas, she tested my patience. She made confounding decisions. Not only has she allowed Eli back into her life, she invited his mother to join us. She didn't check with me first. She pulled me aside one afternoon to tell me that Lauren would join us for the holiday. "It's important that we try being a family," she said.

"We don't have room for her here," I said.

"If Liam's not coming home, she can sleep in his room."

I hadn't meant physically.

Elizabeth appeared more invested in this idea than Eli. Knowing his mother, this didn't surprise me. The boy spent his life running away from home, and perhaps he thought he'd finally found a permanent escape from her in Michigan. But Elizabeth was a benevolent person who hated to see fissures in families. She wanted Eli on good terms with his mother. You never know what could happen, she always says. Eli agreed that we should put the crisis behind us. This is the rationale of a condemned man. It's what a man says when he's desperate for shelter and love after betraying everyone in his life.

"WHAT TIME DO WE NEED TO ARRIVE?" ELI'S MOTHER ASKED over breakfast. We were in the dining room eating oatmeal that Henry had prepared, pretending that it was a formal affair.

"Ten thirty," I told her.

Henry read the newspaper in silence. He couldn't engage with people he didn't respect. He found her imprecise, and precision was the criteria through which he judged other people. In his mind, those who lacked precision lacked the most basic understanding of life. He couldn't respect imprecise people. He had ended friendships over imprecision. People he'd known for years tossed away like wax cups out of bus windows. I found this habit itself imprecise, but after decades of marriage I knew there was no point in telling him this, lest I risk being labeled imprecise.

"That's hardly enough time," Lauren said.

It wasn't even 8:30.

"Is anyone in the shower?" she asked.

All five of us in the house were sitting around the table. "It's all yours," Elizabeth said.

"Have you told her what this is?" I asked Eli, once Lauren left. "It's a modest event. There's no need to dress up."

"She likes to look her best," Elizabeth said, then to Eli: "Isn't that right?"

He nodded. "She's really excited to come."

"I don't want her to feel overdressed," I said.

"Eli's mom is just more invested in traditional beauty," Elizabeth said.

"You act like you come from cavemen," said Eli.

"That's not what I'm saying."

"It's what you're implying."

"It's a good thing to care so much," I said, the vaguest approval imaginable. Henry grunted agreement. Elizabeth gave Eli a look that seemed to say, *See what I mean?*

TWO HOURS LATER, WE ENDED A TIGHTLY PACKED RIDE IN my sedan in front of the main entrance to Landing. Lauren wore a low-scooped black dress and a faux-fox-fur coat and leather gloves. Her makeup was immaculate and simple, a dash of eyeshadow, a few lifts of mascara, a dusting of blush, and a light, unobtrusive lip. These were features I noticed on other women but never allowed for myself. It would be inaccurate to say I was jealous of her but just as inaccurate to say that I wasn't. I did not want to envy her. I wanted to think, *Good for her. I'm glad she continues to protect her appearance.* But I couldn't think this without feeling a pinch of regret over not being the type of woman who cared about my appearance. I knew that I was pretty. My parents had been good-looking, and I had the bone structure of a model. But I rarely *tried* to make myself look even better.

Compliments were beneath Henry. Or perhaps he had exhausted his lifetime supply on the first woman he loved, a tragic and unsurpassable woman I had long ago stopped competing against. Henry valued compatibility and duration. There had been a time, after Elizabeth went to college, when I focused more on my appearance, hoping, in what felt like a shamefully teenage way, to elicit desire from my husband, but he responded to these attempts—which ranged from tasteful to lewd—with devastating silence. I went unnoticed in front of him. Even when I tried, when I was eager and crude, the most he offered were charmless inquisitions about what I was wearing. I sometimes had to beg him to tell me he loved me, that he found me beautiful, and when he did tell me the very things I'd asked him to tell me I would only feel worse, as if I were simply a voice on the other end of an earpiece, feeding him lines. In these moments, and after, my disappointment would devolve into pity: My husband's erotic imagination had atrophied like an unwatered fern.

Would things have been better if I had left my husband for Casey Fitzpatrick? Of course not. But things would have been different, and I had spent countless nights fantasizing about how different my life could have been. We were the people we were. Stability is the cost of stability. This is the life that I wanted. I married the man I wanted to marry. And had I been the one stepping out of the car in a scoop dress, faux fur, and heels, I would have envied the married therapist in black slacks and a navy blue blouse, wearing the world's most discreet earrings and not even a breath of makeup, standing beside a tall man in a faded navy suit, the same suit he wore for every special occasion, his head deftly shaved, erotic.

We did not hold hands. We never held hands. Though I felt an urge to clasp onto him as we entered the auditorium, but before I could he jammed his hands in his pockets.

I didn't doubt that he loved me.

I never doubted his love.

But love was rarely what I wanted from him.

In the lobby, the teenagers were working as ushers and servers, delivering guests to their seats and pouring coffee into Styrofoam cups.

Most of the guests were the patrons of the arts who lived in town, the mothers and fathers of Elizabeth's childhood friends. Some of them *were* her childhood friends. I expected her to mill among them, to catch up, but she and Eli rushed into the lecture hall to wait in their seats. Seeing her avoid her friends filled me with sadness. She must have felt so embarrassed after what happened in Europe, unwilling to tell to anyone what brought her back home.

Henry joined them at their seats. Lauren and I were alone together in line for coffee I didn't want. I felt obligated. I was an excellent and incorrigible host. I was also nervous to see Ellen Locke and knew that drinking something during her lecture would put me at ease.

"This is such a beautiful campus," Lauren said. "Is it right to call it a campus?"

"Henry normally calls it the grounds."

"That's so fancy," she said.

I smiled, irked. She was right. It never occurred to me how it might sound.

Lauren and I hadn't talked one-on-one since her arrival at our house. In Bulgaria, when she and Eli returned to the apartment, Henry and I avoided them both. I didn't want to say anything hurtful to him or his mother. I was not a judgmental person; I was a good judge of character who said what I felt. The concessions she'd made in raising her son offended me. Who could raise a child who treated his wife like he did? I avoided her for her own good. She didn't deserve to hear what I thought.

"Can you remind me who this woman is?" she asked.

"Ellen Locke. She's one of the most talented writers working today," I said. "An absolute and irrefutable genius."

"What are her books about?"

"They're about everything."

"A fitting subject," she said.

"But mostly they're about womanhood and aging and being a mother. The charms and humiliations of growing old in a world that hates women."

"You think the world hates women?"

"Isn't it obvious?" I said.

"It isn't obvious to me."

She asked me to recommend one of Locke's books. "They're selling signed copies. Which one is your favorite?"

I recommended the most recent book, the third in Locke's trilogy, quite possibly the worst place to start with her work.

The coffee line stalled. At the front, Evian Ledbetter, one of the wealthiest women in town—the wife of a local dairy tycoon—was arguing with an usher about the types of coffee being served. She wanted a latte, from what I could tell, made with her husband's milk. The scene embarrassed me, and this added to the embarrassment I already felt for recommending the third book of Locke's trilogy, and, perhaps desperate for some escape from this feeling—how else can I explain what I said?—I confessed to Lauren that I didn't approve of what her son did to my daughter.

"You're very naive," she said.

"Excuse me?"

"You act like I can't tell that you disapprove of his behavior. Like it isn't obvious that you disapprove of me too."

"I'm not trying to start a fight."

"Of course you are," she said. "But you're too proper to admit it."

The line dissolved. Lauren asked for a large coffee and was told there was only one size.

"You don't know better than me," she said. "You only know different things."

I ordered a tea. "I know I didn't raise my child to treat her spouse the way you raised yours to treat his."

"We don't have any control over them. You think you do just because you're closer, because you talk more often, but your daughter is as much a stranger to you as my son is to me."

I thanked the server and made a show of tipping three dollars.

"I don't approve of how he acted," Lauren said. "If that's what you're wondering. Don't ever think that I do."

"That's worth talking to him about."

"Your problem is you find his actions abnormal."

I reminded her that I was a therapist. Everything human was normal to me. I grasped for a Latin phrase but couldn't remember the whole thing and had to cut myself off, pretending whatever I'd said was the entire phrase.

"I also went to college," she said. "Going to college doesn't prevent bad things from happening to a person."

I followed Lauren to the book table because I couldn't pry myself from this argument—perhaps I truly did long for a confrontation, the sort of thing I never had with Henry.

She picked up the book that I'd recommended. "This one?"

I nodded.

The cashier resembled one of Liam's friends back in high

school. The boy was likely that boy's younger brother. He asked Lauren whether she'd read the first two books.

"It's a trilogy?" The question was directed to the cashier but meant for me.

"If you haven't read the first two, it might be best to start with *Schema*, the first one." The cashier passed her a copy of *Schema*.

"I'll take all three," she said. As the boy totaled the cost, Lauren said, "I can't believe you recommended the third book in a trilogy to me."

"You asked me my favorite," I said.

"I like you," she said. "I admire the life you've made for yourself and I wish the two of us could be friends, but you resent me, and I resent you for resenting me, and there's very little we can do about that."

I did resent her. Not for being her but for being the mother of a child who so willfully hurt my daughter, and now I resented her for seeing the feelings I believed I was hiding. "I like you," I said. No one alive would've believed me.

She scoffed.

"What I don't like is how your son acted."

"I don't have to like what he did to continue to love him." She paused, remembering where we were, in a lobby surrounded by locals dressed in gala casual, the real estate agents and bankers entitled to one unassailably elegant morning a year. "Our job isn't to control them or tell them what to do. Our only job is to love them and keep them alive."

"That's so reductive," I said.

"Just say stupid," she said. "Just tell me you think the foundation on which most parents base their relationships to their children is stupid."

I wanted to believe in something more complicated. But I didn't. The love of a parent shouldn't have been any more complicated than what she described. Our job was simply, stupidly, to love them and keep them safe. Complications arose when those two demands were put in conflict; they were only ever in conflict, I feared, when people like me forced them into conflict by thinking too hard. When had I ever tried to do anything for Elizabeth other than love her? Everything I did for her was born out of this principle: love. I let her move home, after all, and let her husband move into the house with us, not because I agreed with her choices but because I longed to keep her safe. The anger I felt toward Lauren and Eli were tied to my impulse to protect my daughter, because in letting him into my house, I worried I wasn't protecting her. My anger was shame. I had to accept there were pains I could never prevent.

"I miss my daughter," I told Lauren. "Something happened to her and I don't understand it—she isn't the same as she was, and I blame Eli for that. How could she do this to herself? How could she forgive him?"

"What makes you think she forgave him?"

"Don't get philosophical."

"After my husband left, I would have done anything to get him back, I pried into his life, I contacted his friends and his family to try to get him to talk to me, and now I hate that man with every ounce of my blood in my body, this man I once begged to return to me after he showed zero remorse for treating me badly, the father of my son, a man who, even when we were married, bored me into a stupor."

"Are you saying Elizabeth hates Eli?"

"For twelve days, I feared Eli was dead, and I'm jealous of what you have now: my child inside your house, your daughter in her childhood bedroom. I hate what he did to her and I've told him over and over again but he brushes it off, insists I don't understand. He's as lost to me as your daughter to you. Don't expect to ever know why he acted this way—I doubt he knows. And you shouldn't expect to understand why Elizabeth let him back into her life. Just accept that it happened and do what you're supposed to: protect her and love her."

"May I see your tickets?" asked the usher.

We followed him up the steps to the row where Elizabeth, Eli, and Henry were seated. There were two open seats: the aisle and the one on the far side of Henry. Lauren took her seat as I shuffled down to sit next to Henry. He asked if I was crying.

"It's about to begin," I said, too embarrassed to tell him I was. The lights dimmed and Henry draped his hand over my knee, and this act of comfort made me cry even harder.

The director of the Landing residency stepped to the spotlit podium to welcome us here. He was a vole-like man in round brown glasses who spoke with a mix of pretension and enthusiasm about the work being produced by the artists. He listed forthcoming books and shows and concerts from recent residents in an effort to convince the guests to donate again before leaving. The director only lived in town on weekends, when he drove five hours from Chicago. Seeing him in the grocery store on weekends weighing bananas in his hands or eyeing flanks of ribeye disarmed me. He didn't seem like the type of person who had a life outside the life he was currently living, standing behind a podium praising the artists our donations could further inspire. Some people are meant for only one thing, for only one life. He was one of those people. Fundamentally, from birth, he was "The Director of Landing." He welcomed the author who would introduce Ellen Locke: Clay Madsen.

Clay Madsen was one of those Brooklyn novelists who wrote about being a Brooklyn novelist. He had begun his career as a poet, a detail that never escaped his interviews in online magazines, because this implied a greater degree of commitment to the craft. Intrigued over the hype of his novels, I checked out his first poetry collection from the library, but the byzantine language reminded me of reading a refrigerator manual.

Madsen took his place at the podium. He wore similar glasses to The Director but was a few inches taller and not so much handsome but intense, like an unattended iron charring a shirt. "It is with great humility that I introduce the esteemed Ellen Locke, a writer whose ruthless aspirations toward truth, the capital-T Truth which only summons the bravest artists among us, has awakened a generation of authors, including myself. The intangibility of her collapsible narratives marks her as the unrelenting messiah of a world that cannot help but contend with its own pretentiousness and failures to communicate. She is an artist of the highest rank, and to speak of her would be to speak of that which cannot be said. With her, we wade through all that can never be named but is inescapably felt."

Someone in the audience clapped. It was a fine place to end an introduction, and I didn't fault the clapper for trying. Madsen kept reading.

"The artist must always create her own reality, and in the work of Ellen Locke the real world, as we know it, is exposed as a farce. Far more real is the reality created by art. The real, her work suggests, is a constructional phenomenon not unlike the unreal." He paused. "This is where Locke situates her fictional reality. If you can even call our reality real after reading her work. But that is why we read her. That is the goal of the artist: to undo and reconstruct one's sense of self by embalming the real with the formaldehyde of language."

Madsen took a drink of water and cleared his throat. I had no idea what he was talking about and needed out of this room—out of my life.

"In capturing the authenticity of the maternal and giving a voice to experiences historically marginalized by the dyspeptic gates of male genius, Locke has created a world we did not know ever existed: our own. I would not be here without her lamp leading me through the darkest tunnels of modern existence, and it is my great pleasure to introduce the only true genius among us: Ellen Locke."

For a long time, I harbored fantasies of becoming a woman like Ellen Locke. I wanted to be ruthless, to be the type of woman—the type of artist—who put my work before everything else. In college, I had written slim, incomprehensible novels in the style of Beckett—imagine!—and in the years since, though I never told Henry, I kept a journal I hoped would one day become a novel. I called it my Magnum Opus. It was the project that would make all of this living, all of these feelings, all of this shallow, everyday pain worth experiencing. I did not want to be like Ellen Locke. I wanted to be better than her—to do what even she couldn't. Locke was notorious for burning bridges, for her very public and contentious first divorce and her even more public second, the novel she wrote about both of those men, turning them into twiggy figures of pity. Her honesty was a cudgel. It was so brash, so empowering. She had been criticized for the things she said about her ex-husbands, the secrets she disclosed, but wasn't that the point of writing? Hadn't she done the very things this Brooklyn novelist claimed? She created real life through the unreal. She revealed how we actually lived.

Sometimes, I imagined a future for myself where I did the very things that she had. Where I would publish my Magnum Opus, my all-too-honest portrait of life likely to humiliate Henry and my own children. I spent my life *waiting* for this moment. But when Ellen Locke stepped to the stage, I did not see an artist made invincible through the act of telling, I saw a woman only two years older than I was who appeared bony and haunted, at once light and entirely heavy, a woman who had lost lovers and friends and who—according to a recent profile—no longer spoke to her children because they were mortified by her depiction of them in her novels. What did she have to show for all of it? Books. Pages. And words. The tiniest things in the world. That's it. Simply a pile of pitiful books.

I felt sickened, then, by both her and my desire to be her. How empty ambition renders a person. I couldn't stand to be in this room, so I exited amid the uproar of clapping. "I need air," I told Henry. Elizabeth and Eli seemed confused as I left. Lauren offered an understanding nod.

THE LANDING GROUNDS HAD NEVER FELT SO DESERTED. I tightened my arms over my chest, wishing I'd remembered my jacket. My breath clouded my face. The sky was as blank as the glass dome of a snow globe. A cigarette would have been wonderful then—though I hadn't smoked since before Lizzy was born—and I hovered at the entrance, hoping one of the ushers might sneak outside to smoke. Muffled applause oozed through the walls. No one was coming outside.

I was too embarrassed to return at this point. Ellen Locke didn't deserve to be interrupted. She was the kind of woman who would not take kindly to an interruption; she was the kind of writer who would spend four pages in her next novel detailing the bland clothes of the woman who interrupted the narrator's speech.

I went for a walk. Later in the day, all the artists currently at Landing would be required to open their studios to show the donors their work. I hated the open studio tours. I hated herding into the cabins alongside the locals asking tedious questions about inspiration. The artists considered me one of the locals—another fool asking foolish questions—because I *was* one of the locals. I was just as guppy-eyed and slush-booted as everyone else. I wanted to hear the artists discuss inspiration. Where had they plucked their ideas from? Which translated to: How might I begin to pluck my own ideas once again?

After half an hour walking the grounds like a lost soul, I settled into a cabin called Everett. I expected a flinch of warmth in the cabin, someplace a degree or two warmer, but the cabin was ovenly. The writer—and the notebooks scattered across the desk made it obvious this cabin belonged to a writer— left a small black space heater running, flouting the rules of the residency. I shut off the heater out of respect for Henry's position.

Books piled twenty spines high created a tower of research on her desk. In the center was a single black laptop clapped shut. A small yellow legal pad served as a mouse pad. I assumed the writer was a woman for no reason other than intuition—and her need for ongoing warmth. In the dresser, I found women's underwear, and in the lower drawers were dresses, blouses, tights, and blue jeans. I retrieved a bulky wool sweater the color of cranberries and pulled it over my torso. The sweater billowed on my frame, but I doubt she was much larger than me. It was a man's sweater. It smelled foresty, like her lover's cologne.

Hung on the wall was a wooden plaque shaped like a shield. All the cabin's previous artists had signed the plaque in black marker. I made a point of not looking too hard at the names, though I wanted to.

I settled at the desk and opened the laptop. Alarmingly, it wasn't password protected. On-screen was the writer's latest draft, the file name *Illegitimacy Ch 31* followed by today's date. I scrolled slowly all the way to the top of the document. It took minutes. But I liked skimming this book in reverse, seeing phrases shout cleanly off the page without meaning. Before I could begin reading from the beginning, the storm door on the porch slapped open and shut. I sprung up, frightened, and slammed the laptop closed, thinking it was the writer returning. I tugged the sweater over my head, but it caught on my arms as I wriggled free.

"It's okay," I heard. "It's me."

I dipped my head back through the neck of the sweater and straightened my hair with my hand. "What are you doing here?"

"I was looking for you," said Eli.

We hadn't been alone together since before he and Elizabeth left for Europe.

"Where's Elizabeth?"

"She wanted to watch the rest of the lecture."

"How was it?" I asked. "Don't tell me."

"Astounding," he said.

"Of course it was," I said.

"Astoundingly awful," he added, a kindness. It was the type of joke Elizabeth would have made, and it reminded me of Henry and I when we were younger, how we adopted each other's mannerisms and jokes, mirroring out of infatuation. In those early days, I loved catching Henry using the same wide-eyed gasp I displayed when feigning shock over something he said, just as Henry seemed pleased when I muttered an elongated *hmmmm*, just like he did, when considering options for dinner. Decades later, I couldn't remember whose mannerisms were whose.

"How long do you plan to hide here?" he asked.

"I didn't even intend to come here," I said.

"You know this is Ellen Locke's cabin," he said.

"Oh my god," I said, mortified.

"I'm kidding."

"You don't know it isn't."

"She would never settle for someplace like this."

I laughed. "Well if it's any old writer's place, we may as well treat it that way." I flopped onto the foot of the bed. Eli sat down beside me. "I'm wearing her sweater," I said, leaning forward to sit.

"It's obvious," he said.

"Is that sociopathic?"

"That's more your field than mine."

I removed the sweater and bunched it in my lap. "I've never read any of Ellen Locke's books," I admitted.

"You love her," Eli said. "She's all you've been talking about."

"I've read all her interviews," I said. "But I'm scared of her books. I'm scared they'll expose something about me I don't want to see."

"Isn't that the point of her work?"

"How would I know?" I said, and we both laughed.

"I think that's the point of all writing," he said. "To show people things they can't see on their own, everything right in front of their faces."

"Did Elizabeth tell you that I wrote when I was younger?" I don't know why I was talking to him—I hated him. Perhaps it was the joke that he made, the one stolen from Elizabeth. Perhaps he wasn't as intense and detached as I believed—for the first time, I saw something delicate in him, something that wasn't tortured but merely confused.

"She told me a little," he said.

"What I admire about Elizabeth is that she's willing to say what people won't admit for themselves. She is fearless. It's what I love about her and what terrifies me. Her autonomy. She's never needed me, not a single day in her life. She was born knowing how to thrive."

"That doesn't mean she couldn't use help."

"I wouldn't know where to begin with her."

"Or that she never wanted help."

"I feel like I'm the child beside her."

"But she's your child," he said. His defense of her further endeared him to me. "I bet she'd want to hear these things from you."

"What things?"

"That you find her impressive and wise. That you admire her."

"If I could say those things to her, then I wouldn't be telling you now," I said. I didn't realize how true this was until I said it out loud.

Eli inched closer to me and clasped my hand with his, and

I didn't wiggle away. He held my hand the same way Elizabeth used to hold on to my hand, when she was a little girl, when I lowered my hand for hers before we entered a crosswalk, sliding her pinky and ring finger into the space between my ring and middle finger, as if her whole hand was an entire finger smaller than mine. She was the only person who'd ever held my hand in this way. There was nobody else. I leaned my head on Eli's shoulder and pulled the bunched red sweater close to my chest, as if I were holding my own heart. A long time passed before anyone opened the door.

# Acknowledgments

I began this book at a cabin in Maine alongside two of my favorite people in the world. Thank you, Mary South and Noah Bogdonoff, for listening to those early draft pages beside the fire—and for urging me to keep writing. Your friendship has kept me stable through too many rocky years.

Thank you to my agent, Marya Spence, who pushes me to be more precise on the page and more mindful in life—you're a five-topping agent! Thank you, Mackenzie Williams and everyone at Janklow & Nesbit.

Thank you to Rakesh Satyal for your ongoing belief in my writing. You've brought so much care and insight to my work. I'm so glad we've been able to work together again. Thank you to Ryan Amato and the entire team at HarperVia: Ashley Yepsen, Lucile Culver, Tara Parsons, and Ashley Candelario (I'm still obsessed with the playlist).

Thank you to my publicist, Kathy Daneman, for all the work you put into this book—and for sharing a perfect cinnamon roll. I will, for better or worse, never forget Switch.

Thank you to my early readers: Julia Fine, Alexander Lumans, and Noah.

This book was written during a time of massive transitions. I never expected to make a life for myself in New York—as much as I always wanted to—and I am immensely grateful for the friends who made living here possible. Thank you for your conversations, your jokes, your long dinners, your hugs, your wisdom. There are truly too many of you to thank by name.

Thank you to my parents for your patience and your support.

Thank you, Heidi. I have no idea how you learned to weather my many writing anxieties, but you've been the absolute best person I could imagine here. You're crisp and complex—not too cheesy—and make for a perfect pairing. I love you.

# About the Author

Isle McElroy (they/them) is a nonbinary author based in New York. Their writing has appeared in the *New York Times*, *The Atlantic*, *New York Times Magazine*, The Cut, *GQ*, *The Guardian*, *Vogue*, *Bon Appétit*, and other publications. They have received fellowships from the Bread Loaf Writers' Conference, the Tin House Summer Workshop, and the Sewanee Writers' Conference, and they were named one of The Strand's "30 Writers to Watch." In May 2021, Isle founded Debuts & Redos, a reading series for authors who published books during the pandemic. Their first novel, *The Atmospherians*, was named an Editor's Choice by the *New York Times* and a book of the year by *Esquire*, *Electric Literature*, *Debutiful*, and many other outlets.

# A Note from the Cover Designer

The cover for Isle McElroy's *People Collide* had to be striking and bold to match the novel's enticing premise. I explored various solutions for cover art but one artist's work in particular resonated most.

Berlin-based illustrator Tina Berning has a portfolio full of figurative, expressive work, and her piece *When It Hurts IV* aligned perfectly. The combination of strong type and considered art complements the many detailed layers in McElroy's writing. An incredible collision of art inside and out.

—STEPHEN BRAYDA

Here ends Isle McElroy's
*People Collide.*

The first edition of the book was printed and
bound at Lakeside Book Company
in Harrisonburg, Virginia, August 2023.

A NOTE ON THE TYPE

The text of this novel was set in Adobe Caslon Pro, a typeface designed by Carol Twombly in 1990. She studied specimen pages printed by William Caslon (designer of the original Caslon) from the mid-eighteenth century. The original Caslon enjoyed great popularity; it was used for the American Declaration of Independence in 1976. Elegant yet dependable, Adobe Caslon Pro shares many of Caslon's best qualities, making it an excellent choice for magazines, journals, book publishing, and corporate communications.

**HarperVia**

An imprint dedicated to publishing international voices,
offering readers a chance to encounter other lives and other
points of view via the language of the imagination.